Minstrel

Bernadette Durbin

This book is a work of fiction. Names, characters, places, and incidents are the product of the author's imagination or are used fictitiously. Any resemblance to actual events, locales, or persons, living or dead, is coincidental.

MINSTREL Copyright ©2016

Line By Lion Publications
318 Louis Coleman Jr. Drive
Louisville, KY 40212
www.linebylion.com

ISBN: 978-1-940938-78-3

Once Upon a Time...

Maybe this wasn't such a good idea after all.

Lydia's knuckles were bleached white in the moonlight. Her arms were already beginning to grow tired. She looked at the windowsill, which was mere inches above her tightly clenched fists , and knew that it was as out of reach as the sun. Her gaze traveled down the makeshift rope to where the base of the tower was lost in the rising fog. She swallowed and closed her eyes briefly. Then, with a whispered prayer, she forced her left hand open.

The jerk as her body dropped was just short of too hard; the fingers of her right hand held. Her grip, at least, was strong. She wrapped her left hand around the rope and eased down as best she could with a jerk that was a little less intense. Her legs twisted involuntarily around the rope and she found that it lessened the strain. The desperate jerks became more of a controlled fall than climbing.

Then, the bottom of the knotted bedding slipped around her legs and she found herself at the very bottom of the rope. Her feet swung freely as she panicked for a moment.The fog was truly thick now. The ground could be just beyond her toes or a deadly length below. Lydia had no way of knowing.

She couldn't climb back up even if she wanted to. Her arms were screaming in pain. *I'll have to drop,* she thought, and began to count. *One, two...*

The ground rushed up to meet her. She hit and rolled, tumbling down the embankment until her feet splashed into the river.

Lydia looked numbly at the end of the rope, still clutched in her hands. *Three?* Then the momentary shock wore off and she swallowed. A look for the top of the tower revealed nothing but increasingly dense fog. She threw the remains of the rope from her and got to her feet, re-settling her small pack on her back.

She stumbled away from the tower, not stopping to check whether the rope had broken—or whether it had been cut.

—

Little Red Cap

Then he sent for his lady gay as fast as send could he,

"Oh where's my son that is sent from me and my daughter Maisry?"

"Your son has gone to the king's high court, earning his meat and fee

And your daughter's gone to the queen's court, a fine lady to be."

"Oh ye lie, ye lie, you e'il woman, so loud I hear you lie!

You've turned my son to the Laidley Worm that lies at the foot of the tree,

And my daughter Maisry you've made the Mackerel of the Sea!"

"The daughter of a Duke never does her own mending," Lydia quoted loftily, biting off the thread and pulling on her newly darned sock. She looked at her covered toes with pleasure. Alas, they *would* keep wearing through.

She tugged on her boots, once fine, but sadly diminished after weeks on the road. The layers of trail dirt made them more than a match for the boy's clothes she had on. She pulled down a ringlet of coppery hair and squinted at it, tucking it back under her hat. Were it not for the hair, one could scarcely credit that she and Richard were siblings, let alone twins. She'd traded away his old outfit soon enough; not only was it too fine, it hung loose on her smaller frame and made her look half her age.

Lydia smiled, and shouldered her pack. "The daughter of a Duke never goes traveling alone." As she set out on the hollowed path, she added, "and it is unseemly, Lydia, to be roaming about the woods with none but a servant for companionship."

Not that there had been anyone to go with her other than the servants. Her father's wife was not given to considering such things. Lydia sighed. The Lady Siona meant well, certainly, with her attempts to polish the quiet girl. It was simply a bit difficult to deal with servants who suddenly would say no more than "yes, miss," and "no, miss." But the beautiful outland lady certainly knew propriety better than the motherless daughter of a dukedom in the far north of the kingdom.

Lydia had spent most of her recent months in the company of her baby brother, Mikal. The nursemaids had treated her with a deference that bordered on awe, but Lydia had scarcely noticed. The child—who would never know their father—was a laughing, golden boy who loved when she played her harp. She rarely spoke to him, but she sang every song she knew and not a few she had made up.

Your son has gone to the king's court, earning his meat and fee, and your daughter's gone to the queen's court, a fine lady to be...

Lydia still remembered the delight she'd felt upon hearing the golden tones the minstrel brought from his harp, and the joy she'd felt when her father had hired the minstrel on to teach the tiny girl. Her first harp, small though it was, utterly dwarfed her, but the minstrel—what was his name?—must have been a good teacher, for soon she was learning to mimic his playing, and to play with some degree of competence. He had even shown her how to read and write music, for so far north, musicians were few and far between.

When Richard was learning skills with horse and hawk and battle, or when winter dark made reading her stories a strain, music filled the lonely hours well. Playing for the family was something only she could do. It was something that always earned praise from her distant father.

She began to craft songs of her own, when the written music ran thin. Rare were the songs with lyrics, for she still felt shy of her voice. The window seat of her tower was a grand place to practice. She could see the laborers in the fields, stretching out before her to the foothills by the sea. She always waved, though she doubted they could see her.

"The daughter of a Duke should not be courting the attentions of the common folk." That quote was bitter, a rebuke. Common folk, indeed. Some days she felt as though they were the only ones who paid her any attention to begin with, since her brother was gone to the capital.

To the capital... Lydia sighed. Now that their father was gone, she knew it was important, for Richard to represent the land,. She frowned a little, wondering. It had saddened her, when her father was killed, but not as much as she thought it should. Not as it was for the girls in her stories.

Then the frown turned to a rather impish smile. The girls in her stories, she knew, had often gotten into trouble through running out of money, bargaining badly or forgetting that *common* folk rarely saw jewels or larger coins. But as part of her upbringing, Lydia had most properly learned the management skills a noble lady should have, and knew what things should cost. Her store of coin was still quite adequate.

She'd had the coins stored away, not for any real purpose, but because it made her feel better to have a stash. She had never expected to need it. She shivered, then, as the memory of why she had needed the funds intruded.

Richard had sent her a new horse, a bay mare, and her enthusiasm had caused smiles all over the keep, where they didn't think she'd see. Even the new captain of the guard, a dour man who frightened Lydia, had widened his pressed lips at her joy. But Lydia knew the guard schedule well enough that she could sneak out, her candle unlit, to groom the horse herself, and care for the tack. When she had been handling the saddle blanket, she'd felt something hard under her fingers. She'd brought it over to the candle she was using for light and saw the glint of metal in the weave. It took a few minutes to realize that what she was seeing was a popjack, a child's toy— a thin piece of metal that was shaped like a dish but could be pushed inside out, and which eventually righted itself. If you inverted it, and placed it on the ground, when it turned itself right it would pop into the air.

When Lydia had pushed this one, sharpened metal barbs sprung out of the weave. She let it go, and with a little click it popped back. She had pressed it a few more times, thinking carefully. This would be worse than a burr under the saddle. A rider's weight would move this back and forth indefinitely, until the fractious horse bucked in pain.

And that was what had sent her out of her tower window that night, to flee south to the capitol, where Richard was. Richard was the only one she could trust now.

*   *   *

Lydia felt chilled. It was hard to articulate exactly how... *trapped* she had felt at the keep. There was no person who spoke above a few words to her aside from the Lady Siona. Even the nursemaids for Mikal had done barely more than nod their heads as she came to play for the baby. And Lydia had long since finished her formal education with the priest.

Until the night in the stables, she had seen no threat. But it had felt as though she were caught in a slowly closing net, the places that she could go getting closer and the things she was allowed to do getting fewer. She had felt almost smothered. After the first few nights, when she feared a pursuit that never came, she found herself far more relaxed than she had been in months.

Almost too relaxed, she began to consider. True, she had bargained well, but after a mild season, folk were unsuspicious and welcoming. What if the winter had been hard? Her woodscraft was minimal, at best, and she only knew enough to avoid the toadstools. It was early spring, so there weren't any berries, but weren't there roots of plants that should be good?

One of the old servants might have told her, had she asked. But then, she'd never realized she might need to.

She'd seen rabbits, but she had no idea how one set a snare for them. Deer were obviously beyond her reach and—come to think of it, while there weren't many predators down in the farmlands, she had seen foxes, quite close, and seemingly unafraid of a person on foot. If a larger creature... a wolf, or a bear... were so unafraid, Lydia wouldn't stand a chance. She swallowed, but moved deeper into the trees. She would find a safer place to stay that very night.

In her worry, she didn't immediately spot the man standing in her way. He moved, very slightly, and she jumped. His clothes were fine, but well worn, and somehow they did not fit as though they belonged to him, suspiciously mismatched. His hair was uncovered and greasy, and he watched her with eyes as flat and uncaring as those of the captain of the guard.

Lydia swallowed. He was a very large man.

"Good day," she said, and started to veer around him, but he grabbed her shoulder and forced her to stop.

"Give it, then," he said, in a voice surprisingly beautiful, a light tenor that could have charmed the birds out of their trees. His breath smelled of wild garlic. Lydia shied back.

"Give what?" she quavered, her voice rising dangerously. He frowned, peering at her face in the shadowed light. Then he pulled her hat off, and her hair, in its long braid, tumbled out and down her shoulders.

His smile was ugly. Without warning, he backhanded her across the face. Lydia fell, her possessions scattering as her pack fell apart. He held her down and when she struggled, knocked her head against the ground, his hand around her throat. She continued to struggle weakly but was dazed. *My father was killed by brigands*, Lydia thought wildly. The man—the *brigand*—began to tear at her clothes. She flailed at him to no avail; he brushed her hands aside as though they were flies.

Part of Lydia wanted to do nothing more than whimper and curl into a ball. Another part—the practical one—had her feel about for something, a rock, or anything to give weight to her blows. Past the trembling in her hands, she felt something hard move under her fingers, and when she grasped it, it fit her hand.

She put all her strength into a blow at the man's head. Her arms were far too short for that, and she hit him square in the throat with her knife, her little eating knife that had fallen loose from her belt.

The brigand widened his eyes in a brief moment of astonishment before the blood came surging out of his throat, and all over Lydia. Then he collapsed, his weight pinning her atop her possessions. Her struggles against a dead weight were different than against the malicious weight of before; while she didn't have to fight, he seemed heavier. For a moment, Lydia imagined that his corpse was trying to press her down into the netherworld.

That gave her the strength to finally worm her way out from underneath the brigand. Her ears rang and she panted with the effort and the aftershock. She finally turned around and saw the corpse of a man in what had once been fine clothes, slowly bleeding into the earth. A keening whimper slipped out between her teeth. She bent over and vomited.

Lydia's breath whistled in her throat as she sat back, panting. She started to shudder, looking firmly over the corpse. A horrible sticky awareness began, and she looked down at her clothes, which were torn, disheveled, and covered in blood. *Not mine*, part of her thought, *not mine. It might have been*, she realized, and covered her eyes.

Her hands were as horrifying as the rest of her. She pushed them against the ground—still tacky with blood— and stood, a little shakily. She began to gather her pack, piling everything she owned (and not a little bit of dirt) on her bedroll. She avoided looking at one patch of ground.

But she hadn't had time, and she needed everything she'd carried. She walked over, cringing, and shoved at the corpse's shoulder. He barely moved. She pushed a little harder, and then crouched down. All of her weight was barely sufficient to turn him over.

There was dirt sticking to his open eye.

Lydia clamped her teeth shut and held a hand over her mouth as nausea rose up in her again. Working quickly, she gathered up those last few items that she had fallen upon. Last of all, she took the little knife (*A lady's knife*, said the voice of her father in her mind) from his throat.

I'll have to get a new one, she thought distractedly, and then realized that she might not be able to. She bundled up her blanket of belongings and stumbled off without looking at the corpse.

*   *   *

One hundred strokes every night with a boar-bristle brush, its ivory handle yellowed throughout the years. The hairbrush had been her mother's, one tiny legacy to a daughter who didn't remember her. One hundred strokes, and then careful braiding that her hair might fall in graceful waves. The Lady Siona had condoned her nightly ritual, mentioning only that her maid ought to attend to the strokes.

Lydia much preferred to ready herself for bed alone, and smoothed her copper curls over her hand. She sometimes lost count and continued the strokes, dreamily imagining fair knights and gallant princes. Other times, she looked in her small mirror, unable to see just how the hair fell from her forehead. It never seemed quite the same in the larger mirror downstairs, whose backing gave everything a slight bronze cast. But she knew that her hair, which, unbound, fell to the backs of her knees, was copper that fired gold in the summer sun.

One hundred strokes for beauty, she thought, as she looked at the hair on the blanket before her. Lydia bit her lip.

She had managed to get the blood out through vigorous washing. Lydia had scrubbed in the icy river water until her nails turned blue. In the end, though, she only had the one knife to cut her hair off at her shoulders. She rubbed the cut ends between her fingers. It was a rather ragged job.

Sunlight fell all around her but failed to warm beyond her skin. Her clothes were still wet and drying on her body, roughly repaired. For a wonder, she had thrown her embroidery into her pack the night before she'd left. The needles, more precious than coin, meant that she could do a few simple things, such as stitch up... damaged... clothing. She rubbed her hands on her arms.

I could cry now, she thought. *I could yell and scream and there is no one to notice.* But instead she just looked at her hair, copper-gold, beautiful waves against a simple blanket.

*   *   *

She did not sleep so well after that; fear of predators both human and animal made the hard ground seem even harder. The towns came closer together and busier as she drew near the city. Buying food became a chore now. The farmers she met talked a little differently, and Lydia was far too aware that her accent, however slight, marked her as a foreigner. Not, perhaps, so outlandish as the Lady Siona, but someone to be watched with suspicion nonetheless.

The first night that she couldn't find a piece of forest to sleep in, she awoke from a nightmare of large, looming shapes. She didn't think she'd cried out, but while she tried to calm her heart she kept a wary eye out for those who might try to track down the source of her screams.

The second night, she didn't even bother trying to get back to sleep, but packed up in the dark and began to walk again by the light of the waxing moon. She didn't stop until the moon set.

Between the extra walking and the nightmares, she didn't notice at first when she actually reached the city.

Lydia finally realized that she had been expecting towers, or a wall, not this gradual beginning of living space. But there it was ahead of her; a series of buildings built upon one another, using the existing stones as a ready wall. The area thus enclosed was small, and would have permitted no more than a town. The city had long since expanded beyond those boundaries, and the houses and shops were stone, brick, and timber.

A few wary cats watched her as she slowed. She'd gotten here. She had finally reached the capitol.

Lydia suddenly realized that she didn't know what to do. She had left the keep with one thought in her head: to get to Richard. She'd walked the whole distance without considering quite... how... to get to him. He was in the palace.

She was in the city.

And she was dressed in boy's clothes, badly mended, with ragged hair... and no sigil. She had no rings or tokens or proof of her identity. She swallowed a breath. Perhaps... perhaps she could try anyway.

By the time she had walked through the increasingly rich parts of town, with the servants of the nobility stirring and glaring at her as she walked down the streets, and turned toward the palace with its liveried guards and heavy gates swung wide, her courage began to fail. She saw how the guards examined every visitor, noble or not.

It was only a few minutes before, shuddering, she conceded defeat and turned around, making her way back toward the poorer parts of town. She would have to find another way to get a message to her brother.

The Peacock Prince

River, oh river, carry my troubles away
My love has turned false,
she is bound to another;
oh river, dear river, help me as you may.

River of sorrows, river of grace,
Sweet gentle water to cover my grief,
River of mercy, save me a place
Be my companion and grant me relief.

Late Winter (the following year)

Thin sunlight barely seemed to light the roads, turning the cobbles a nondescript gray. There seemed little difference between them and the bleak sky above. It was almost as though spring fought to overcome this tail end of a winter whose unrelenting cruelty was more in its unchanging nature than with the cold that still worked its way into the castle.

At least one of the party that rode out of the castlegates had a mood as gray as the weather. The riders that followed him were speaking with some animation but he rode in silence. His clothes were scarcely richer or better cut than that of the others, yet it was evident that they respected his mood, and did not press him. The guards who shadowed the procession watched over him closely, far more than they watched over the others.

That is the price one pays for becoming a king.

William's nature did not tend toward melancholy, but the winter just past had rained one misfortune upon another. The early joy at the mild weather had turned to regret when signs of rebellion had started to show, and the lack of snow had done nothing to make the miseries of cold-weather campaigning more palatable. Far worse was the raid in the night, the one that the rebels must have known would fail, but which led to fighting in the dark, and a death toll that should never have happened.

Worst of all was how the king, his father, had survived battle only to fall prey to a fever that swept the camp and later, the city

William didn't feel kingly. He also didn't feel entirely secure. Those that surrounded him seemed loyal enough, but as he well knew, that was no good indication. He was a young king, and naturally a happy youth, but one well-trained in his responsibilities to the running of the land. Now, he was the one his people looked to for the settling of quarrels, and of disputes among the baronies and fiefdoms that comprised the country. He was the dispenser of wisdom and of law.

It terrified him.

So he rode out, with a group of nobles—don't call them friends—in an attempt to escape the circling thoughts of winter. At an earlier hour than most of them were accustomed to, there was very little traffic on the streets. Here a trash-picker, leading a mule; there a drunk, half-roused by the sound of hoof beats, saved from a frozen death by the recently gentled weather. The stores and stalls of the market had not yet opened. Most waited until the warmth of the day to bring in customers. William sighed, a counterpoint to the wind which now wrapped around timbered buildings instead of stone.

Though not entirely aimless, the wanderings of the horses quickly took the party well off the main thoroughfare. One of the noble youths made some deprecating comment which led to general laughter; William roused a bit and noticed that they were in a part of town which seemed, somehow, dirtier and more worn than the parts he was familiar with. He was about to turn the party back when his attention was caught by a strain of music. Harp music.

The unexpectedness of harp music in the slums froze him still for a moment, and when he had listened for a bit, the familiarity of the music caught at his heart. Determined to find the source, he directed the guards closer, and after few turns, they found the harpist.

He sat on the very edge of a doorstop at a prouder building than most in the area. His clothing was an indeterminate gray from wear and dirt, and all but rags. Rags were the only cover for his feet and the palms of his hands; his fingers were left free to glide over the strings of the harp with utter certainty. A shapeless hat flopped over one eye, but even had it not obscured his vision, William doubted that he would have noticed the horses approaching. The harpist played as though the music were the only thing keeping him alive; as William eyed the narrowness of his face and the protruding cheekbones, he began to wonder if that were indeed the case.

The sound of hoof beats finally roused the harpist and he turned in surprise, fingers faltering. His eyes grew very wide at the sight of the noble group, and he scrambled to his feet, clutching the harp as though it were a talisman. When they approached a little nearer, he bowed to the company at large and then to William in particular. Then he suffered a minor fit of coughing, turning his face so that he did not see William's surprise.

"You play very well," William said when the coughing subsided. Though the face was respectfully lowered, William could see the boy's eyes widen briefly.

"Thank you, your majesty," he replied, very softly, as though to speak louder would reawaken the coughs. William dared not show surprise that a common lad would know him on sight; the chance of his face being seen at anything other than a distance was very slim. The accent was slight, and foreign; perhaps he was some traveling minstrel's assistant, left behind by the death of his master.

Lost in speculation, William wasn't quite sure what to say, and the lad obviously did not dare speak out on his own. His trembling hands gripped the harp—old, battered, and little finer than its owner—a little closer to his chest. One of the horses shuffled, its hooves muffled by the half-frozen mud of the street. Carl of Eastoak, impatient, asked what business they had in the area, unless they were going into the brothel. A quick look at the proud building only revealed its better repair, though its carved shutters bespoke a certain indolence. Eastoak looked entirely indifferent.

Interesting, noted the king. *I live in this city, and I had not known a brothel when I saw one.* He looked at the harpist below him, and for lack of anything better to ask, said, "Do you live here?"

The lad jerked as if he had been slapped. "In the brothel, sire? No, I have no... business in such a place."

"Playing to get coin to get in, then?" sneered Eastoak. When the boy turned a look somewhere between astonishment and affront, Carl rode over and cuffed him on the side of the head. "None of your looks, *boy.*"

"Leave off, Eastoak," William said quietly. The boy held his flaming cheek and looked steadily at the ground between the horse's forelegs. Eastoak sniffed, declared his intention to be bored no longer and rode off, trailing one or two of his particular friends. William motioned for one of the guards to follow them, then turned back to find the harpist hadn't moved.

Unsure what to do, the king fidgeted for a moment, then asked, "Will you play something, then, for us?" Immediately, the lad looked relieved, and sat back down on the stoop.

A pause, then a quick bend to the strings. In a moment, a simple melodic phrase gave way to a complex beauty that seemed far beyond the abilities of such a battered instrument. The tune hovered on the edge of recognition, and for a moment William thought he recognized it. A traditional ballad, a daughter—or was it a son?—turned to a dragon, to be freed—how? William didn't remember. But then the tune spun away, into something different but still maddeningly familiar.

As before, the music pulled the player away, and William felt pity move the bleak depression a little. The song wound down, and the boy exhaled, gently, and laid his thin cheek along the harp.

The rest of the nobles were quiet, from respect of the music or at least of the king. William didn't care much. He asked, "What is your name, boy?"

He looked up, then, widened eyes meeting William's for the first time. They were strangely calm as he said, "It is Alan, your majesty."

That steady stare unnerved the king. He went on, "And what reward do you ask for such a song?" Instead of stammering, or surprise, or even calculation, the lad merely gave William a quizzical look, and shook his head mutely. William looked back; the assembled nobles were regarding the harpist boy with looks ranging from annoyance to amusement. One of the older ones, more sympathetic than most, said, "Hire the lad; he can sing for his suppers." William looked at the squad leader of the guards and received no shake of the head in return. The boy was not considered a threat.

"Well then," William said, "Will you come and play for the king, Alan?" The past months' frustrations and trials prompted him to add, "I have no minstrel." Behind him, he heard a sharp intake of breath.

Alan licked his lips and closed his eyes briefly, then lifted them to his monarch's. "If that is your will, sire." His tone was hopeful, but afraid of wanting too much. William smiled, and the lad almost flinched. A little disturbed, the king motioned the squad leader forward. "Done, then."

He looked at the boy a moment longer, thinking to say something, but Alan was staring at the ground. A moment's conversation with the squad leader had him selecting one of the guards, who nodded. The company rode off, and only the guard remained to look at the boy who was staring into space, as though he could not believe what had just occurred.

After a moment, the guard dismounted. He knew better than to take an untrained—and perhaps frightened—boy pillion. Alan reminded him of a feral animal, or perhaps an unbroken horse, which is probably why Captain Dar had selected him for this duty. Though the boy didn't look at the guard as he walked up, he leaned away, as though he might run at a moment's notice.

For a moment the guard just looked. The lad—youth, rather, he was older than his size would lead one to expect—was holding his harp like a shield. The layers of clothing he was wearing masked his extreme thinness, but did not seem to be keeping him warm. The guard reached into his saddlebag and withdrew a roll. He handed it over, merely saying, "It's a long walk."

Alan swallowed and seemed to focus on him for the first time. He took the roll and levered himself to his feet, then looked at the bread in his hand. A grimace passed fleetingly over his face, then he tore off a small piece and began to chew. The guard observed the cautious maneuverings that were required to keep hold of the harp and eat the bread at the same time, and did not offer to take the instrument.

Under the shapeless hat, the hair was a shade that might as well be called dirt. Dirt or bruises marred the narrow face, occasioning another frown from the guard, who had little use for people who abused the weak, whether they be animals or men. The lad walked not as though his feet did not hurt, but as though it did not matter that they hurt. His skin was pale and while the guard had no doubt that he was cold, he did not offer a cloak. Wild animals are easy to scare. Besides, the guard and the minstrel were of such different sizes that a cloak could only be a hindrance.

The guard was a normally silent young man, but after they had walked several blocks in silence, it occurred to him that an introduction might be in order, at least. "I am called Sean." He opened his mouth again, and the youth actually looked at him, but when he could think of nothing to say, he closed it and continued in silence. Once he got too close to Alan, who flinched away. Sean tightened his lips.

The youth was nearly stumbling by the time they had reached the castle gates. He had finished the bread and still clung to the harp a little too tightly. Sean paused at the gates, where the guards on duty merely looked down in inquiry. "The king has hired a minstrel," he said, indicating the youth, who leaned against the horse. "His name is Alan, and I am taking him to Melinda."

The guards looked at the lad carefully, that they might know him again later. Alan seemed alarmed by such scrutiny, but was too unsteady to have more than a moment of fear pass through his expression. Sean passed his horse off to a stable boy and dared to place a hand on the lad's shoulder. He looked ready to collapse, and while he twitched when the guard touched him, he did not pull away.

A faint attempt at a smile answered the guard's questioning gaze, and Sean took the most direct route to the kitchens, where Melinda was sure to be at this time of the morning. The minstrel froze in the doorway, shocked by the busy bustle of the room. When Sean attempted to draw him in towards the large hearth, he only shook his head for a moment, then seemed to realize what he was doing.

"It's—it's the harp," he stammered, seeming to focus on the guard's face. "If it gets too warm..." He looked a bit helpless, then jumped when a voice behind him said, matter-of-factly,

"It won't do the harp good, will it? There's a shelf over here where you can set it for now."

The lad turned to see a woman only a little taller than himself. She was sturdy, capable, and wearing an apron. She indicated a shelf with a wave of her hand, and Alan bobbed his head in thanks. He set the harp down carefully, and then used the key that hung from a piece of twine at his waist to quickly turn the knobs loose.

The woman leaned over toward the guard and asked quietly, "Is the king taking a charity case?" Sean shook his head, and murmured, "The lad is very good, Melinda." This reply did not seem to entirely please her. She placed a hand on Alan's back and guided him toward the fire, gently pushing him down on a bench almost too near the blaze. He merely sat in total exhaustion.

Melinda stood back and let her eyes rove over the lad for a minute or two, then she motioned for two maids and sent them off on her errands. "Now, then, lad, what do you go by?"

"Alan," came the terse reply. He didn't seem to have the energy for a prolonged conversation. Melinda frowned, briefly, before she fetched a cup of hot broth from a side hearth. "Drink this, Alan." Somehow it was more of a command than a kindness. "I've sent Lindy off for some decent clothes and Maisry to start the baths. We'll get the livery later." This garnered a bare nod. Melinda placed her hand on the harpist's cheek, finding the thin layer of heat from the hearth turned to ice in the fire's shadow. "Drink your broth, lad."

The "lad" nodded her head. From Lydia's perspective, the whole incident had the flavor of a fever dream. The kitchen had no windows on this end of the room, and most of the light was cast by the flickering fire. The insistent woman kept telling her to ingest liquid fire, and she somehow didn't have the strength to leave the place where she was slowly being roasted alive.

When William had ridden up that morning, at first she thought that he must be a hallucination. It was too perfect, to storybookish, for the prince—no, the king—to rescue her from the flat gray chill her life had become. She had been half convinced that she was dreaming until he spoke, and she realized that he hadn't recognized her at all. That irony alone had brought the reality of the situation to her.

Her habitual pose as a boy had been so well ingrained by then that she had managed to keep up the charade, and the wonder of it all was that he had, in a way, rescued her.

It hadn't been so bad at first. She'd realized early on that she needed a way to replenish the money that was, despite her thrift, leaving her purse far too swiftly. The harp had been a lucky find, as the minstrel had been willing to part with the ugly instrument to another player for a price that was only slightly too dear. In the summer, coin had been easy to come by as traders and fairgoers visited the city.

But with the turn of the seasons had come the loss of custom. Lydia had long since taken to climbing into haylofts instead of renting rooms. The deepening winter saw the gradual loss of the insulating hay, and a few times an angry stableowner had turned her out. She began skipping meals, hoarding her few coins until the seasons turned again. She had given up hope of contacting Richard, hearing vaguely that he had left the capitol again.

Her boots had given out. She gathered rags and wrapped them around her feet until they might possibly grow warm. Missing meals turned into hungry days, and the worst part wasn't the hunger. She'd expected that, and in fact there came a point when the constant dull ache became so normal that she could try to ignore it.

The worst part was that being hungry made it so hard to *think*. She had the attention span of a mayfly, and resented it; her thoughts had so long been her only companions that she missed them desperately in their absence. It was as though her last friends had deserted her.

Her fingers started to fumble and slip, and she occasionally grew careless with her secrets, which grew larger as the winter rolled on and the turmoil began. The effects were little felt in the city, though the rebellion had its strong partisans. Lydia took care to not be seen as one, something which stood her well when the rebels were put down.

But she had played well enough that morning. The sudden shock of William's appearance had given her the energy to sustain that momentum until now, when she was seated before the fire.

She decided that, on the whole, fainting would not be a good idea. In her starved and frozen state, it took her a long time to reach that conclusion.

"Lad." Lydia jerked; she had been dozing, and almost spilled the dregs of her broth. She looked at the mug in some surprise. When had she finished that? She looked up at the woman—Melinda, that was it, her brain *could* still work on occasion—and tried to look attentive. Gradually, Melinda swam into focus, holding a bundle of cloth out. "We have some clothing for you—no shoes yet, more's the pity—and Maisry will show you to the baths. Can I trust you not to drown yourself?"

Lydia had to think this one through. She realized that she was almost warm for the first time in far too long, and the shock started her shivering. But she nodded, and said, "I won't fall asleep. I think." And suddenly the whole ludicrous nature of the situation hit her, and she added, "I do know how to wash behind my ears."

Melinda smiled, suddenly. "If you survive, then, I will have a meal set aside for you, because breakfast is long gone and dinner is not for hours." She stepped back and looked Lydia up and down. "It will be small, because you can't eat much now without getting ill, but any time you are hungry, come to the kitchens and the cooks will feed you." Once again, it had the flavor of a command, one that promised dire consequences for the hungry lad who avoided food. Lydia shook her head in wonderment and followed the maid.

The baths were a large room with a blazing central hearth, and several tubs of varying sizes in alcoves with curtains. One of these had been filled partway full with hot water; Maisry indicated the cistern for cold and a kettle for hot, and a bucket for transport. She then looked at Lydia with something like pity and something like anticipation, and said, "It will be good to have music again." At Lydia's surprise, she added, "There are several places just outside the hall where the sound carries well." Then with a smile, she left.

Lydia bit her lip. At the midday, it was unlikely that anyone would come; this was probably also the servants' baths, so no worries on that score. The water in the tub seemed excessively hot, and the bucket was heavy, though she prudently only filled it halfway.

When she finally closed the curtain, the near-darkness was in line with her unwillingness to look at what cold and hunger had done to her. But the bath—just a little too hot—finally melted the ice at her core, and stopped the occasional shivers.

She scrubbed as best she could, discovering that chapped skin could only take so much abuse. The heat had begun to leach out of the water by the time she felt moderately presentable; the air, by comparison, was cruel. She rubbed dry as quickly as possible, then dressed in front of the fire. The new clothes were simple, but fairly well-sized; perhaps they were the hand-downs of some page who had hit a growth spurt. Her bare feet were, at least, clean.

The heat of the fire began to wake up her mind a little, and certain realities occurred to her. While her chest was starved away with the rest of her, eventually she'd need some binding. She looked at her rags with distaste, then shrugged and grabbed some to wash in her bathwater. If she couldn't find something better, these would do. Somewhat regretfully, she ran her hand through her clean, though short, hair. Clean it was, and relentlessly red, too. That would never do. Not now.

A handful of soot from the fringes of the hearth and a little water, and her hair was dulled down. Again, she'd have to find a better solution.

When she stepped out into the hall, she found Maisry waiting there, to her surprise. The maid looked satisfied with what she saw, and Lydia wondered what would have happened had she been insufficiently clean. No doubt Maisry would have dragged her back in and scrubbed her herself. She might have been able to swear the maid to secrecy, but Lydia just didn't know. Maisry pulled out a set of soft slipper-like shoes from behind her back and handed them to Lydia, who accepted them gratefully.

`"You'll get proper shoes later, but these should fit for now," Maisry said.

Lydia considered for a moment—far too slowly, because Maisry started to look concerned—then replied, "Thank you." Another pause, then she went on: "I haven't had anyone to talk to in a long time." This was accepted, and Maisry led the way back to the kitchens.

Melinda, it appeared, had enlisted the entire kitchen crew to fuss over her. One cook gave her another mug of something warm—tea this time, as Lydia found when she managed a sip—and another showed her to the "best seat in the kitchen," which turned out to be a cushioned rocking chair that was pulled near the large hearth. Yet a third gave her a roll split with honey. Lydia didn't have to be warned to eat that slowly; she wanted to savor it as long as she could.

When Melinda appeared, Lydia noticed that the kitchen had rearranged itself around her. It was nothing so obvious as the cooks moving; it was merely a shift in attention, a certain restraint, an increase in industry. It might be that Melinda were someone whose approval was hard to obtain, but worth having. Melinda had changed into something newer and finer, almost to the level of a noble. She strode over to where Lydia sat and took her hand and turned it over. Chapped skin protested a bit, but Lydia found herself almost too weary to care. Melinda wasn't going to hurt her. She could read people at least that well.

"I suppose your feet are like that, too?" asked Melinda.

Lydia nodded, then replied, "Yes, mistress."

The woman smiled. "It's just Melinda, lad. Tomorrow, I'll have a salve for you, and you shall get your livery and meet with the Master of Protocol. For now, you are going to bed." At Lydia's confused look, she went on. "Maisry or Lindy will show you to your room."

"I get a room?" Lydia burst out. She'd expected a bunk in the servants' quarters, and had already begun to worry about the difficulties of keeping up the masquerade.

"Of course you get a room, lad, you're a minstrel." Which explained little to Lydia, but Melinda acted as though it had. "Now I must be off."

"Where are you going?" asked Lydia. Melinda was dressed so finely, she couldn't imagine. Melinda's kind smile was warmer than the sunshine. "Why, to the Master of Protocol, to explain why he won't get the new minstrel until tomorrow." And with a flare of her skirts, she swept out of the room.

Lydia gaped after Melinda. Paige, the cook who had given her the honeyed roll, laughed at the expression on her face. "She's taken a shine to you, Alan." Lydia swallowed and took another gulp of tea. "What... is she, anyway?" she asked.

Paige looked thoughtful. "You mean, what does she do?" Lydia nodded. "She... well... she started out as the Maids' Mistress, then started planning meals, and managing stores... I guess she mostly fills the role of seneschal."

Another of the cooks laughed, and said, "She's *Melinda*. Even the king defers to her." Paige turned a frown on the flippancy. "He listens to her, sure, for she manages the castle, but he does as he should. He's the *king*," she said in the same tone as the other cook. She looked at the fading minstrel. "I'll get Maisry."

The obliging maid led Lydia through an astounding number of corridors, up back stairs that hurt her feet through the slippers. The room that Maisry led her to was not grand, but was warm; one wall appeared to be the back of a kitchen chimney. A hasty cleaning had evidently been done; there was a small chest, suitable for sitting on, and a table. Her harp stood on the table, considerably better looking than she had last seen it. Her startled brain finally comprehended that someone had sanded and polished it, no doubt one of the maids used to cleaning furniture. Well, that certainly wouldn't harm it.

But it was the bed that drew her, its covers turned back. She didn't undress, merely sat, pulled off her shoes, and crawled in. Maisry snagged the warming brick with a towel, then pulled the covers over her.

Lydia was asleep before she left the room.

*   *   *

She stirred a bit when the bells rang, tolling the hours, but such a familiar sound did not disturb her much, even close at hand. Exhaustion and the release of the need to be wary propelled her into a deep, dreamless sleep. The sun was setting when she awoke, groggily, to find that someone had been there and gone, leaving a pottery mug full of soup, covered by a plate holding another honeyed roll. She stood, a bit shakily, then walked to the table, where she ate the roll and drank the soup in short order. The plate had kept the soup warm, and had warmed itself as a result.

Then Lydia all but crawled back into the bed, thinking vaguely that it was like being ill, this lassitude. She barely cared that she was in an unfamiliar situation, or that she'd slept the day away and seemed likely to sleep the night as well. Something nagged at her, something she ought to do or remember, but she fell asleep again before it rose to the surface.

When she finally roused fully, it was to the light of dawn on her face. She was instantly alert in a way she hadn't been the day before, a legacy of life on the streets. It took her several long moments to comprehend where she was and why she was comfortable. She sat up slowly, trying to comprehend the change in her status.

The room was small, far smaller than her tower room at home. That might have annoyed her in a previous life; now it seemed almost welcoming, and comforting. The sunlight came in through a window that was actually glazed, though with small circles of pressed glass. Some of the palm-sized panes were the gold of ripe wheat; a few were of a vibrant green. Kentwell's colors. Lydia chose to take that as a good omen.

The hangings on the walls were clean but worn and told of amateurish attempts at embroidery. They also were strong in the gold and green motif; small doubt that they were in here precisely because of the window. The blankets on the bed were a gray wool, though the sheets were of tight-woven linen, precisely stitched together.

Lydia sat, covers pulled over her lap, and thought of nothing. It was the first pleasant waking she'd had in months, and she reveled in it. When the door moved, she twitched only a little.

The maid at the entrance was hardly cause for alarm. She was overburdened with not only a pitcher, but basin and mug besides, as well as a covered plate of some kind. The pockets in her apron bulged with other implements. The maid herself was rather colorless, with dingy brown hair and a sallow complexion. Lydia stared at her as she maneuvered the assemblage into the room. The maid looked as though six hands would not be enough, and yet nothing dropped.

After depositing the pitcher, mug, basin, plate, and a towel on the now crowded table, she looked over at Lydia where she sat in the bed. "I'm Lindy, Master Alan." Her voice was timid and shy, but she spoke as one who is determined to discharge a duty properly. Lydia slowly crawled out from beneath the covers, inwardly mourning the loss of their warmth. Unsure of what she was to do, she sat on the chest at the foot of the bed and looked at the maid, who promptly poured her a glass of water.

Lydia took the mug and swallowed; the cold water hit her stomach like a slap and her eyes went wide. "Basin," she croaked, and slapped a hand over her mouth. Lindy took the hint and deftly grabbed the bowl, holding it in place as Lydia retched. Once her stomach was emptied of what little it yet contained, Lydia leaned, listless, against the edge of the table. Her good mood gone, she felt like crawling into a hole and pulling the entrance in after her.

Cool water bathed her forehead; the maid had wet the towel. Lydia opened her eyes and looked miserably up at the maid. "Are you done?" asked Lindy soberly. A moment's thought, and Lydia nodded. A glance at the maid told her that the shyness had been replaced by sympathy, and Lydia managed a wan smile. Lindy held out the towel, and Lydia took it gratefully, mopping her whole face and finally her nose.

Lindy looked over at the covered plate. "That's your breakfast, if you've a mind for it." She began divesting her pockets of an amazing assemblage of objects: a wide-toothed comb, a piece of parchment and a graphite stub, a tinderbox and, amazingly, not only tallow candles but the holders to put them in, a palm-sized mirror, scissors...

An eating knife. Lydia's stomach did a slow roll.

The maid picked up the scissors; small, they might have once been from some lady's embroidery kit. "I'm to trim your hair." Lydia turned around, wordlessly, and barely moved as the maid began to comb out her hair. She had forgotten about the soot but the maid had no comment. Lindy probably thought it was just dirty.

The maid took no small amount of time on Lydia's hair, enough so that the stirrings of appetite had a chance to reawaken. Finally, she handed Lydia the tiny mirror and said, "There. You don't look so messy now."

Lydia looked at herself in the cold light of day. She could barely see the haircut by turning the mirror this way and that, though it did appear to be even, cut just above her shoulders. It, too, was dingy, a grayish brown that spoke of nothing more than ashes. Her face, though, was very changed from what she remembered.

Her cheekbones stood out in sharp relief, and her chin held a sharp point. Dark circles under her eyes looked like bruises against her winter-pale skin; several other bruises across cheek and forehead matched quite well. Even her eyes appeared to be drained of color; she thought they had been brown, but looked little more than gray now.

Small wonder she hadn't been recognized. She looked like a wraith.

"Less messy," she managed.

Lindy nodded. "You are a fright, young master, but we'll feed you up." She pushed the plate over. "D'you think you can manage this?"

Lydia uncovered the plate to find a slab of cooked meat, still warm in spite of the delay, a cup of porridge, and a hard-boiled egg. She looked down at Lindy. "I can understand that you're feeding me up," she said, "but does it have to be all at once?" Lindy, who had started fussing around Lydia's feet with the parchment and the graphite, looked up calmly.

"Melinda's orders, Minstrel Alan," the maid said as she traced Lydia's feet. "You're to eat all you can, especially the egg. It's good for you." Lydia did, slowly, while the maid finished fussing about her feet and started fussing about the room. By the time the maid had installed all of the candles—and why on earth,

Lydia wondered, was she to need quite so many—Lydia had finished all of the porridge, and the egg, but hadn't touched the meat, or the knife needed to cut it.

Lindy, still expressionless, looked at the meat, then at Lydia. "Doesn't it smell good?" Lydia shook her head; everything still had the faint smell of sick from her earlier episode, and she didn't want to provoke another. She still felt weak, and wanted nothing more but to crawl back in bed—an indulgence, she felt, that would not be granted to her today.

Lindy loaded up the plate and the pitcher, and balanced the basin atop gingerly. She had barely left when the door opened again. This time it was Maisry; Lydia wondered if she was the especial charge of these two, or if this was merely their wing of the castle. Unlike the colorless maid who had just left, Maisry was all suppressed excitement... had she been the previous day? Lydia's memories were a blur.

"I have a present for you," she said without preamble, and held out a small pottery jar. Lydia took it, puzzled; Maisry went on, "It's that salve Melinda promised, for your hands and your feet." She watched while Lydia, still seated, broke the paraffin seal and scooped out a fingerful of faintly herb-smelling goop. Without saying a word, she smoothed it between her hands, where it did soothe the chapping and the chilblains. Then, as Maisry still said nothing (but looked a bit mischievous), she scooped out more and rubbed it on her feet before working them back into the slippers.

As she placed the jar most carefully on the table, Maisry grabbed her hands and pulled her to her feet. "Come on," she said, as Lydia, suddenly scared of going outside, resisted. Lydia relented, and allowed herself to be pulled into the hall.

What followed was a whirlwind tour of the castle, at least those parts dedicated to the servants. Every servant that they passed was stopped, and introduced to "Minstrel Alan," while Lydia tried very hard to fix names to faces in her mind. Every room was pointed out, with notes as to whose it was, or to what purpose it was put, and poor "Alan's" mind was awhirl. This was several times larger than her father's keep—as well it should be, she reminded herself—and held more than three times the people.

Every guard was likewise introduced. Lydia was not so overwhelmed as to miss the pity that showed on many faces when they spied her bruised and overly thin face; nor did she miss the amusement that they showed at Maisry's enthusiasm. Maisry even *flirted* with some of them. Lydia goggled; flirting with guards was something she never would have considered back at the keep.

She wondered if she would forever be comparing her new life to her old. This thought set her jaw.

When the tour looked to be ending, but barely half the castle gone over, Lydia did ask about the rest. Maisry looked a little troubled. "Over there is the chapel—they have morning prayers, which you've missed, and the Lord's Day services. Behind that is the noble's wing... and to the right is the wing with the locks." Lydia's confusion showed on her face. "The prisoner's wing," Maisry explained, "where they keep the nobles who've done wrong. They don't just throw them in the dungeon, you know." And Maisry's expression, for the first time, took on a tinge of anger. "They've got him there, the traitor who wanted to kill our king."

Lydia was deeply shocked. "I thought he was killed in battle," she ventured. Maisry shook her head. "You were out on the streets, right? I know there were rumors, but he was captured, not killed, and brought back for trial. They'll cut off his head before the lilies bloom." She eyed Lydia carefully. "You're to stay away from that wing, you hear?"

The ringing bell punctuated Lydia's nod, and Maisry grabbed her hand again, half-running to the kitchen, where she all but shoved Lydia into the rocking chair before dashing off on some other errand. Lydia shortly found herself in possession of a plate with yet another slab of meat—possibly the same one from breakfast—another mug of broth, and yet another hard-boiled egg. For a moment she sat, bewildered, with her hands full and no way to eat. Then with a shake of her head, she collected herself and set the mug on the floor between her feet.

"Can you find your way back to your room, then, lad?" a voice came from behind her, and Lydia jumped. Melinda walked into view. "The way that child shows people around, I'd not be surprised if you couldn't." Lydia thought a moment, then nodded; her sense of direction hadn't deserted her, and she could well find her way back. Conscious of Melinda's eyes on her, she rolled her egg on the edge of her plate to crack it. Hard-boiled eggs were a treat and not to be wasted.

Melinda nodded. "Good, then. Finish your food—no need to rush, but don't dawdle—and head back. You'll find some livery up there, and some light shoes to match. We'll have the cobbler come by in a few days to put you in better shoes. Then a page will take you to Master Orrin."

Lydia swallowed the last of the egg. "Page?" There hadn't been any pages that she'd seen.

For a wonder, Melinda understood. "The pages get instruction in the morning. As will you."

This was reassuring rather than otherwise; Lydia had been afraid of too many missteps with her new position. Melinda chivvied her out the door soon enough, leaving Lydia to try to retrace the groggy steps of the previous day. Though the hallways seemed both longer and shorter than she recalled, and the steps less numerous, the route was quickly deciphered.

Once back in her room, she changed as swiftly as she could, lest the page come in unawares. The livery consisted of an undyed linen shirt, rather fresher than the shirt of the previous day (and which Lydia now recalled she had slept in), black knitted hose, and a tabard of cardinal red embroidered with the royal coat of arms. She belted it only enough so it wouldn't slip over her hips; there was no need to call attention to the fact that she was excessively thin.

The outfit was surprisingly warm, and she fingered the quilting on the tabard, wondering if there were a summerweight option. This far south, that might not be a worry—last summer had seemed very cool to her, but the townsfolk hadn't acted as though it were unusual. The linen cuffs were simple, though perhaps a bit long, and might get in the way of her harp playing.

The knock on her door came as she was adjusting the hat (red and black, with a copper brooch.) She startled and the hat fell to the floor, whereupon she scooped it up and opened the door.

The page was only a little shorter than she was, though years younger; the size of his hands told her that he'd be a veritable giant when he got his full growth. His livery was similar to hers, though on a much plainer scale, and his shirt was black as well. He looked at her gravely, took the hat from her hand and placed it gently on her head.

"If you please, Minstrel," he said, voice hanging on the edge of cracking. "Master Orrin would like to speak with you." Lydia nodded, unsure of what to say, and the page smiled at her and turned, glancing back to make sure she would follow.

She followed, a little nervously, and cleared her throat. "Uh... Page?" The boy stopped, turned around, and grinned. "I'm called Jankin."

"Jankin."

"After m'father. And for my size."

Lydia looked again at his huge hands. "Indeed," she said. Then she shook herself. "Jankin? What should I expect?"

"Expect?" Jankin shrugged and continued down the corridor. "Master Orrin's a good sort, truly, and keeps us all to the mark. You'll do well."

Doing what? Lydia hoped that the protocol master would be more forthcoming. The page eventually led her to a low office in what she thought was the noble's wing, and opened the door, bowing slightly to her as she passed. "The minstrel's here, m'lord."

"Jon," came a well-modulated tenor voice from a shaded chair in the full sun. "I have told you, time and again, that you must work on eliminating that mumble from your speech."

"Of course, Master Orrin," the page replied carefully.

"I think I shall ask you to recite poetry for me next week. Take care to learn some." The speaker leaned forward, and Lydia could see that he was a well-groomed man in his mid-thirties. His clothing—a rich brown with red and gold trim—could only be described as "precise." He waved a dismissal to the boy, who gave a creditable bow and left, closing the door behind him.

Master Orrin placed his hands on the table. "Minstrel," he said. Lydia swallowed. "Yesterday, Melinda told me that not only had the king hired a minstrel, he actually hired him off the street. She also told me that the boy was ill-used and needed rest. Have you had that rest?"

Lydia started to nod and realized that more was needed. "I have, Master Orrin."

He stood, then, and walked around his desk. He was only of average height, a fact which made Lydia intensely grateful. She did not feel up to being stared down upon. He looked at her carefully, then leaned back against his desk, a casual pose which seemed in no way truly casual. "Bow," he said.

She did, one hand on her chest. He asked her to bow several more times. "You shall bow whenever you enter the king's presence, and when you leave; you shall bow for visiting dignitaries and for functionaries. You bow to any noble that you meet in the corridors. As you will be playing the harp at gatherings, you should bow to the company at large before beginning. Your bow is adequate. I expect it will improve when your health does."

Lydia looked up at him from her latest bow. That last bit had almost sounded humorous. Orrin motioned her over to a wooden chair of simple but graceful lines. She sat, and wondered what was to come next.

The protocol master proceeded to quiz her on an amazing number of subjects, beginning with the various keeps and duchies and baronets in the kingdom. She thought at first that she might dissemble but the questions came so quickly that she was answering to the best of her ability, scrambling to keep up. Lydia was rather appalled to find that there were a number of places she had never even heard of, let alone heard of their lines and alliances, their goods and their responsibilities.

The questioning then moved to more esoteric subjects, like history, math, and rhetoric. She had a general idea of the history of the kingdom, and was more than competent in math, but she had never even heard of rhetoric. Orrin wrote a few notes on the parchment in front of him, and Lydia tried to suppress her rising dread. Surely she would still be acceptable. A minstrel needed to know music, not history or this rhetoric.

She was fairly certain.

Her eyes moved to a map on the far wall. The sun was no longer full in the windows, and the map almost sparkled in the reflected light. It was a map of the kingdom, in brilliant colors she had never seen in inks. Perhaps it was painted.

The protocol master followed her gaze. "That is a teaching map. It is, perhaps, somewhat out of date." Lydia nodded, reflective rather from any real knowledge. As best as she could recall, she'd remembered every grant in between Kentwell and the capitol, but nothing south of there. Yet the kingdom stretched on for another eighty leagues south of Ellidar, including a long stretch of shore along the icy Suthron Sea.

Orrin wrote a few more notes and then motioned her to rise. "I think I shall undertake your education myself," he said, and Lydia sucked in her breath. "You are advanced in some areas and not in others and it would do you little good to be in the general courses with the pages." She hadn't expected this.

For a moment, she was confused. What did she expect?

She bowed, and said, "Master Orrin? A question?"

He waved a hand. "What—exactly—am I to do?" she asked.

The protocol master leaned back. "Ah. I had wondered when you were going to ask." He carefully wiped his pen clean on a cloth, and laid it on the table. "You are to come here every morning after the second bell. I will undertake to teach you those niceties that you will need to know in order to function in a high court. I shall also teach you such things as the young nobles learn, so as to improve your mind. The king shall call for your music as he wishes. For now, I am told that you shall play in the evenings, for the king's meal."

Lydia flexed her hands. So. She would play before an audience. Master Orrin noted the gesture. "Do not overplay your fingers. I think that you may well be playing every day but Lord's Day."

She nodded. "I understand." It had been a long time since her fingers had hurt with playing, but it was warmer inside. She reminded herself to use more of the salve when she got back to her room.

*   *   *

Dinner had been a simple affair for the servants, set a little before the courtiers' meal. Paige said that in deep winter, when dinner was earlier, the servants would eat afterward, but when the weather warmed up they didn't dare have the servers faint from hunger. Lydia was grateful, though she couldn't eat much.

She reminded herself firmly that she had played before the crowds at the Festival of Folly, at Lady's Sorrow, and the weekly market. Somehow, this last didn't comfort her.

When she presented herself outside the hall, she found that one of the guards at the door was the one who had brought her to the castle. Sean. He half-grinned at her, and whispered, "Luck."

"Thank you," she murmured back. She tugged at the frills on her wrists and straightened her shoulders, pretending a confidence she couldn't feel.

In a few minutes, she reflected that her worry had been entirely unnecessary. The gathered company had barely even glanced in her direction as she gave a general bow, and then one to the king. A flicker of a smile had passed across the king's face, but as he was speaking with his neighbor, an older man wearing the colors of Guardron, she could not know the smile was for her.

As for the harp—it seemed improved, somewhat, for the good treatment it had received, but it still lacked the resonance of a higher-quality instrument. Its strings of twisted gut were barely adequate, but she had not had the money to replace them. The notes seemed muffled in the echoing hall. She winced as she remembered the buzz of the harp the first time she'd played it. The method she had used to fix it made the notes sweeter, but the volume was lost.

Her fingers did hurt more than they had in the numbness of winter, but they were less stiff and the tunes came easily. She deliberately slipped into an easier style, sparing her fingers. As the dinner guests began to leave, she allowed herself to stop, flexing her hands.

A shadow crossed over her, and she looked up to see the older gentleman. She stood and bowed as best as she could—Orrin was right, she was still stiff—and said, quietly, "My lord."

He looked at her carefully. "Do you not sing, then?"

Lydia flushed. Many ballads were repetitive; she'd had to design new parts in order to cover the lack of words. "I am afraid I do not, my lord."

"It seems you should be able to learn." Ah. This was the man who had suggested she sing for her suppers. He might well have been literal.

"My lord, I have a good ear, and it tells me that my voice is completely... unsuitable." That was true enough; her soprano was out of the question and her range was narrow enough that the low notes graveled out if she attempted to sing the songs in a lower register.

The Guardron man made a non-committal noise and walked away. Lydia sank back down on the stone bench, nerveless.

*   *   *

Lydia was quickly lulled by the daily routine. She became used to waking at the dawn bell and getting under the feet of the cooks before morning prayers and breakfast. Besides Paige, there was Pansy, and Rosamyn, and Marta, the head cook, and a veritable army of helpers and servers who seemed shy of talking to her. Maisry always seemed to turn up to fuss over her, and Lindy would take care of everything in her quiet, competent manner.

After breakfast, she would report to Master Orrin. He'd set to teaching her logic, which was apparently the beginning of rhetoric, and quizzing her on lessons he read to her from a large book of history. He'd raised his eyebrows when, frustrated with his slow pace, she'd asked if she could read it for herself, but Lydia hadn't noticed that, or that he'd written more of his cryptic notes as he watched her race through the text. She mostly remembered that the pace of questioning had, if anything, increased.

She'd also discovered within half a day that the servants set to cleaning the castle after lunch. She took her baths at that time. It was the baths, more than anything, which felt like luxury to her. She hadn't been able to pay for hot water since leaving her father's keep, and one could barely stand to keep clean in ice-rimmed water.

After eight days, it seemed as though she had been in the castle for months. A moment of crystal clarity came upon her, and suddenly aware of her position, her fingers fumbled on the strings. She quickly covered by starting a newer piece, one she had developed in snatches over the last few frozen months. Cheeks suddenly flaming, she ducked her head so her features could not be seen. She looked nothing—and everything—like Richard. It would be ill luck indeed if someone were to chance on a resemblance, some shadow in bone and blood that reminded them of him.

For the last half-year, she had been so focused on survival that she had all but forgotten who she was. She'd been taken off the streets so quickly that she only now realized what her new position meant. Here, in the castle, there were people who might recognize who she was.

And in that sudden clarity, she peeked out from between the hair that fell across her face. What had she expected? Certainly more people than the subdued group of nobles that barely filled a quarter of the great table. And the table itself was not large enough to fill the grand space; there must be tables, or even trestles, in storage. And her harp—her lonely little muffled harp—barely reached the table. Lydia looked up at the musician's gallery, empty and dark.

The prince—no, the king—was supposed to love music. Wasn't he?

Lydia knew well enough that there should be more people. Was this, then, the result of the rebellion, or of the old king's sudden death? Or was it merely the result of winter and the hardships of travel?

Her glance darted to the Lord Guardron as he coughed. There was one who would not let something as trivial as the weather discourage him from his duty. She trembled a little at the thought of his piercing gaze. He was from the duchy nearest her own and it was only a small mercy that he had never visited in her memory.

She stared at the highly polished floor tiles in deep blue, vivid cerulean, and cream. To avoid thinking about what she would do once her ruse was discovered, she began connecting them in her head, stars and snowflakes and fantastical creatures. The hand on her shoulder came as a surprise.

"They're gone, Minstrel," said the server, and Lydia looked up to see that he was correct. The hall was emptied of the nobility and held only a few servers and maids, cleaning up the remnants of the meal. Lydia took one long look at the gallery, and then nodded.

*   *   *

"Paige?" she asked the next morning with a mug in her hands. "Why is it that I'm the only musician here?"

The cook's chopping stopped for a minute, then resumed with careful strokes. "Well, Alan, the rest of the music players we had were just here for a short time. They left as the seasons turned and their hires ran out." She bit her lip. "I guess you'd heard that the young king likes music. He hasn't... I mean... we've been worried." The last was said in a rush.

"So," Lydia turned the mug in her hands. "Was it the death of his father, then? Or," she took a quick drink to wet her suddenly dry mouth, "–or was it the rebellion?"

"He hasn't wanted music since the Lady Lydia died."

What?

Somehow, she managed to hang on to her mug. "Of Kentwell?" she managed, with only a little catch in her voice. Paige misunderstood.

"It does seem strange, doesn't it. But Prince William—the king—fell in love with her." Paige sighed, a little regretfully. "It was like a story, you see. It was the circuit year, and they say she was like a dove in spring."

Lydia remembered those days, barely a dream compared to her recent life on the streets. The Lady Siona had coached her through a half-dozen official dinners and the formal dances. Lydia had played for the traveling court and to one pair of shining eyes above all. She hadn't known if it were love, though she always knew where he was in the room.

They had never been left alone together, though one summer evening he'd slipped a flower into her hand. At fifteen, that had seemed the height of romance.

And then they had gone, and her father had traveled to the capitol, possibly to arrange a betrothal. But he had been killed on the route home, and Richard had succeeded him. And that summer was impossibly long ago.

Paige stirred from her own reverie, put her knife down, and faced Lydia, saying gently, "She played the harp, you know."

Oh.

"I understand," Lydia said softly. She could feel the pieces aligning, making sense of a glance here, a comment there.

Small wonder that William had not recognized her in the ragged waif he'd taken off the street.

One question suddenly occurred to her. "How did she die?" Marta and Pansy looked at each other. "A fall," Pansy commented. "From a horse," Marta added.

"I'd heard she drowned," said Paige, troubled. Pansy shrugged, and went back to kneading dough. Lydia remembered a child's toy in her hand, and her feet in the icy river. *A fall, indeed. Or drowning.*

She raised her mug to her lips, signaling an end to her questions. For now.

*   *   *

Her lesson that morning was difficult. On one hand, the text was fascinating—an account of the raids on the southeastern coast, and the somewhat ingenious means that varying towns used to keep them at bay—and on the other, Lydia kept losing track of what she was reading as her thoughts went wandering regardless. She was startled when Master Orrin's hand slapped down on the book in front of her.

"Attend, minstrel," he said, quietly, as though he had not made her jump. "You are distracted."

Lydia swallowed. This composed, thoughtful man was beginning to intimidate her. It might have been the mentor aspect, but she suspected it was largely because he seemed to see right through her. It might also be that she still didn't know why she needed an education, much as it appealed to her.

Orrin sat back in his chair. "So explain to me that which distracts you."

She stared at the desk. "It's... it's hard to explain," she stammered through a mouth suddenly dry. "I don't even know what to ask."

"Ask?" One elegant eyebrow rose.

"Something's wrong here. It's a new reign, a young king..." She spread her hands. "Where are the courtiers? The ambassadors? Why are there so few allies?"

He regarded her as though she were a fascinating new creature, some exotic animal caught in a far country. "This distresses you?" Lydia managed a nod. He laced his fingers. "I think you are overly worried about the situation, young Alan. Most of these... allies... are discharging duties to their lands after a hard winter. No," he said to her look of surprise, "the winter was not overly hard here. But the rains here were blizzards in the south, and floods in the north. There is much damage."

"Most," Lydia said, musingly. Orrin smiled, a slight curve of his lips.

"Most," he agreed. "Most, but not all." And with that, he bade her return to her studies, that next time she might know the questions to ask.

*   *   *

Lydia borrowed a book of history and began to spend her afternoons in the kitchens as well, reading or practicing her harp as the mood took her. Paige would usually hand her a honey roll the moment she walked in through the arch, in return for a smile. She wondered where the hives were kept. Various other cooks would hand her bits of vegetable or bread if she had a hand free, with the result of Lydia eating almost constantly without even noticing.

Melinda would come through the kitchen periodically, smiling benevolently at the minstrel in the corner. Lydia knew that her bruises were fading fast, now that she had enough to eat, and that her increasing health gratified the lady. Once or twice she caught a speculative look on Melinda's face, which worried her, but as nothing seemed to come of it, she shrugged it off and returned to her book.

She hadn't been able to read anything for far too long, and history was interesting enough to catch her attention. She finished the book in a matter of days, and exchanged it for another. Master Orrin showed her the library, which was situated across the hall from his study. The sight of the hundreds of books quite took her breath away.

Orrin began to intersperse his questions with comments on how, for example, the siege of Guardron affected the level of banditry in the Manaro Pass, and how that led to the cooperation of two neighboring keeps, which led to the creation of the barony of Sasden. Lydia soaked it all in with the same love of stories that had led to her collection of storybooks.

The truth of these stories made them even more fascinating.

Lydia did not realize that the speed at which she was absorbing information was of great interest to Master Orrin, who looked on her as a prodigy. Some of the speculation in Melinda's gaze was caused by the speed at which she turned the pages, and by her rapt study of the text. But Melinda said nothing, content with the knowledge that the minstrel had not only adapted quickly, but seemed to be thriving.

For her part, Lydia felt as though the days were an idyll, a respite from those horrible months on the streets. The people around her seemed glad—glad!—to have her company. It was as though she'd descended from her tower to find those farmers and riders that she had always waved at, and they were as bright and cheerful as she could have hoped.

She still had nightmares on occasion, but she had almost grown used to them, used to starting up in the dark, heart pounding and throat dry. She could calm herself by lying back on the rush-filled bed, and stroking the feather-filled pillow. Nightmares and pillows, she felt, had nothing to do with one another.

Some part of her knew that such a state could not last. The court became sparser still, and the entire castle was tense. This time, Lydia didn't need to ask why.

The knock that came on her door that evening, almost three weeks after she'd come, almost caused her to drop her candle. She shook her head and placed it carefully on the small table before opening the door to a guard. She was alarmed for a moment, then realized that he wouldn't have knocked, were it anything bad.

It was worse.

"He's asked for music, and the king has granted the request," said the guard. His face was unfamiliar. "Will you come?"

So.

Not trusting her voice, she nodded, then picked up her hat and placed it on her head with a now well-practiced flip. A tight grip on her harp ensured that her hands wouldn't shake, and she followed the guard to the northeast wing, the one with the locks. They went past many empty rooms and up several flights of stairs. He gestured to a wooden bench placed outside a door with a barred window. With some relief, she realized that she would not be expected to enter the rooms.

Be honest, she admonished herself. *The cell.*

She sat on the bench, the only light from two lanterns flanking the door. The guard nodded and slipped back the way he'd come. Lydia stared after him, wishing she could follow. But she had a duty to discharge.

She started off simple, a ballad that was popular when she was a child, then segued into a splintering complicated variant to get her fingers warm. Without a pause, she continued into another tune, throwing music into the silence, hoping she could play forever.

But she had already played throughout dinner, and soon her fingers faltered on the strings. She stopped, flexing her hands, and froze as she heard movement on the other side of the bars. He must have drawn a chair right up to the door.

"You play like my sister Lydia," said Richard, the traitor.

Rosemary, Thistle, and Thorn

High on a hilltop, where sky meets the green,
I'll dance the Wild Dancing as you've never seen;
I'll dance the Wild Dancing so vivid and free,
And I'll dance for my love who was lost to the sea.

There's grass on the hillside; there's fish on the reef;
There's rocks in the shallows where he came to grief;
There's rocks in the shallows and sand on the shore
Where my love's fading footsteps will walk nevermore.

It was only a door. Richard's low, murmuring voice slipped effortlessly through, yet it shielded Lydia. The corridor darkened, the light from the grille, throwing lines across the ceiling. She longed to reach through the bars, find comfort, and to speak her own name.

And yet, she dreaded it, deeply fearing this brother whom she knew no longer.

The door pressed on her, the word *Traitor* ringing in her ears. It should apply to Richard, but Lydia felt the guilt as a palpable thing, and shrunk from it in horror. It was as though there was blood on her hands, and suddenly, she envisioned Richard with her knife in his throat, and started choking on the blood...

Lydia sat up in bed, heart pounding, to look around the darkness of her room. Richard was dead. No. *Executed* two days gone. There was no one and nothing to link him to her.

Some days she felt as though he were still there, the twin she had always followed and adored. It felt as though some part of her had died with him.

Some part of her had still believed he was innocent.

She began to construct in her mind scenarios, ideas where Richard was somehow justified...

No.

No. He was a traitor. He'd befriended the prince and then attempted regicide. She couldn't make excuses for that.

He was her brother. Her *twin*. And utterly alien to everything she believed in. She desperately tried to calm her mind, to go back to sleep, but her thoughts spiraled back upon themselves like snakes gnawing at their own tails. Dawn found her still awake, empty eyes staring at the ceiling.

Sleepless nights turned to restless days, and instead of studying in the kitchen as she had, her feet took her on unconscious wanderings. She could not seek out Melinda's advice, as that worthy had gone to midwife a niece in town, and she did not want the advice of the cooks, or Maisry. When she drifted into an unfamiliar part of the castle, there was nothing to do but look around until she found her way again. As most of the castle was still unfamiliar to her, this happened all too often.

Upon mistakenly entering the part where visiting nobility was housed, she was knocked down by a stocky man barreling around a corner. He proceeded to yell at her, loudly and quite maliciously, maligning her birth, her parentage, and her clumsiness. Lydia stared at him in wonder, since his outrage seemed far out of proportion to the offense of being in his way. This only infuriated him, and he grabbed hold of one shoulder and dragged her to her feet.

Instead of yelling further, though, his voice dropped into a hate-filled whisper. "You dare not stare at me that way, minstrel. A brothel-born guttersnipe had best watch himself." Then he slammed a fist into her gut and stormed off.

Lydia gasped for breath for a minute, then straightened up slowly. There didn't seem to be anyone else in the corridor, and she looked around, trying to get her bearings. She finally—though slowly—determined from the angle of the shadows where she must be, and tried to wind her way back to her room. She was a bit hampered by looking around corners first, so as to not run across any more outraged young nobles. She did make it back to her room without further incident.

Her luck ran out after that. The outraged noble—whose colors were a pale blue and a bright yellow, unknown to Lydia—had apparently been in need of someone to torment, and a distracted minstrel fit the bill. Whenever Lydia was looking for someplace to be alone with her thoughts, she seemed to find him. In search of a victim, his better knowledge of the castle stood him in good stead. Most of the slanders went right past her, as inaccurate as they were, but the punches and slaps were a more pressing matter. The noble was always careful to hit somewhere that would be covered by clothing, and Lydia didn't dare seek help that might be all too revealing.

She might have stuck to her rooms, but Maisry kept offering to talk, and questioned her far too much for comfort. Once, she'd caught Lydia limping, and Lydia, in a voice creaky from disuse, protested that she'd merely twisted her ankle. The maid's sympathy was enough to drive the minstrel away again.

Maisry became frantic. The minstrel appeared to be fretting himself into the condition he'd arrived in. He had dark circles under his eyes from lack of sleep, he was skipping meals, and once she'd seen him staring at his reflection in the bottom of a polished pot. "He looked as though his heart would break," she told Paige. They agreed to apply to Melinda when she returned.

*　　*　　*

It had been some eleven days after the execution, and the court was returning. Ignoring the recent death, with all-too convenient excuses that had called them away so they need not witness the death of one of their own.

In some cases, hiding from the idea that had circumstances been only a little different, their heads might have been on the block.

William had been badly inattentive during the formal dinner to introduce him to the Duke of Vensport's daughter, but not so inattentive that he'd missed how she never said anything without glancing at her father first, nor how the Duke watched her like a falconer might watch a dove. In the aftermath, as the minstrel played quiet tunes on his harp in some minor key, the Duke himself was in a conversation with the king that the king was heartily bored with.

He was trying not to sigh, or worse, yawn. He really didn't want to marry the Duke of Vensport by proxy. He let his eyes wander around the room and noticed that nearly everyone had left, and the servants were starting to clear the tables.

He was developing a profound dislike to the Duke when a small sound of protest reached his ears. "—will *not*," came the minstrel's voice, and the music came to an abrupt stop with a jangle of strings. One of the unfortunately ever-present minor nobility— Roland? Ronald?—had grabbed the minstrel and pulled him out of his alcove. The harp dropped to the floor with a small *crack*, and William winced. *The man must be drunk*, he thought in confusion, but the only expression on Roland's face was rage.

The minstrel stumbled to regain his balance. Roland cocked his fist back and swung his body's weight into the minstrel's face. Alan fell and his head bounced off of the polished tile. The guards had already started moving, but Roland grabbed for the harp, lifted it, and threw it to the floor, where it shattered instantly.

"Wasteful," the Duke of Vensport murmured. William looked at him, horrified; the jangle of strings and the splintering of wood were still echoing off the walls. The Duke caught something in the look and rose to his feet, indicating that his daughter (who still barely looked at the king) should follow. "You have business, your majesty," he said smoothly, even as the guards restrained the enraged noble. "We shall, perhaps, discuss things tomorrow." He stepped back, bowed, and left the hall. The few other laggards, including Roland's erstwhile friends, took one look at the king's face and made their own quick apologies before departing.

William stood up and walked over to the still struggling youth. He did not address him, but the guards. "I believe the Baronet of Chardon has neglected his lands long enough," he said quietly. His foot crushed a splinter of harp, and he looked down. For a moment, he thought his heart had stopped, but he dragged his eyes up and continued. "See that he gets his possessions together for a speedy journey."

Roland looked up, his face suffused with rage. "Your majesty, that, that—*whoreson* insulted me!" He faltered, looking at the steady expression on the king's face. William said nothing as Roland stammered his way through excuses that must have sounded feeble to the man's own ears. He merely indicated with a jerk of his head that the guards were to take the Baronet out. He watched as they almost dragged the man out of the hall, his outrage at the minstrel quickly transferring to outrage at being handled like a parcel of meat.

Only after the hall was empty did he bend. It must have been hidden in the soundbox, this braid of coppery hair. There were splinters of wood amongst its strands, and one of the strings of twisted gut was tangled in it. William bit his lower lip.

He would have known that shade anywhere.

"I had rather," came a quiet voice from near his feet, "that you burned it, than cradle it as you do." William jerked and looked down at the minstrel. He'd propped himself up on one elbow and hand, and his unkempt hair fell across his face. He spoke to the floor. "You think too much on the dead."

Instinctive protest rose in the king's throat, and died. "How did you get this?" he asked. The minstrel gave a bark of laughter that trailed off into something rather like a whimper. "Why, sire? So you can mourn Lady Lydia all over again?" He struggled up a little straighter. "You waste time on her when you should be finding a wife."

I loved her!" cried William.

"*Did* you?" came the reply, almost wistful. Then, even quieter, "Did you even know her?" Again, a protest shot to the king's lips, and he paused, remembering the Duke of Vensport, and the Duke's daughter. He thought back to the slim days at the keep, the dinners, and the dancing, and how the lady had been paraded before him, as though she were a mare sold for breeding.

And then something in the minstrel's tone caught him, and he said instead, "*You* knew her, did you not." There was no reply, and he looked up to see the minstrel slumping where he sat.

One of the guards reentered the hall and stopped dead at the tableau of the king holding the braid, the shattered remains of the harp, and the minstrel, collapsed on the floor. In a few long strides, he strode over to the minstrel, pulled back one eyelid, then scooped the minstrel up into his arms. He barely nodded at the king before running out of the hall, calling for Melinda.

William stood, silently, until the maids came in to start cleaning up. He was still holding the braid in his hands.

*   *   *

Before she even opened her eyes, Lydia sensed that the room was wrong. The light came from the wrong direction and the bed felt somehow... backwards. In the moment before she fully awoke, she thought that if she could capture the feel of the way the room should be, she would be there in an instant, back in her tower, back in her father's keep.

The thought terrified her into wakefulness. Eyes still closed, she realized that she was in the castle, not the keep. But the room was still wrong, and there was someone in it.

She opened her eyes to the sight of exposed beams had been polished to a dark glossy shine, and dried flowers hung from the ceiling. Tapestries in interwoven patterns of flowers and herbs graced the walls, and a small hearth blazed in one corner. And the bed... the bed was very comfortable, with a featherbed atop the rushes.

The person at the hearth straightened up, and Lydia breathed, "Melinda." That lady did not seem surprised, but came over to lay the back of her hand against one side of Lydia's forehead. Melinda's hand was still warm from the fire. The heat sent Lydia's head throbbing.

Melinda sat down on a chair next to the bed. "Look at me, lad." When Lydia did, she nodded, and said, "You're awake, then, really." Then she put her hands on her hips and said, "Why didn't you tell us?"

Lydia was suddenly aware that she was no longer wearing her livery, that a soft nightshirt covered her instead. She stammered, "I didn't know who to trust... it's—it's so much safer to be a boy..." She trailed off. Melinda was chuckling softly.

"Not that, *lad*. I figured that out some time ago." Her voice grew gentle. "I've seen it before, you know, and you are right. Sometimes it is safer. I remember where you were found, though I've tried to ensure the stories didn't get out." She shook her head. "The bruises. Why didn't you tell anyone that that horrible man was hurting you?"

Lydia looked at Melinda helplessly. "I don't know," she murmured.

Melinda stood and threw her hands in the air. "The Lord protect us from martyrs. Look, you, Maisry has told me you're hurting for something. You can't go putting yourself in harm's way because you think you deserve it. And you can't go starving yourself to death, it would be ungrateful." She stopped and looked Lydia in the eye. "Your cycle hasn't started again, has it."

Lydia flushed bright red, a throb that set her aching head to pounding. Mute, she shook her head.

"I thought not," said Melinda. "You're too thin. I thought I made it clear that You," she said, punctuating herself with a poke of her finger into Lydia's chest, "Need. To. Eat."

"Yes, Melinda."

"And no more soot in the hair. It does horrible things to the bedding." Lydia's flush climbed even higher. "I have some walnut juice that will do for dye. I know that redheads are unpopular now." She sighed and looked at the trembling girl. "I have been hoping you would trust me—or Maisry, or somebody. I didn't think it would take a beating to get you to talk." Melinda paused. "Look at me, lad."

Lydia did, and said, "You call me lad."

"It's a reminder," Melinda said absently, and covered one eye with her hand, and then the other. She frowned a bit. "The king wants to see you."

Lydia sat up straight, then winced. "See *me?* Why?"

Melinda laughed, and pushed the girl back down. "Not this instant, *Alan*. I want you to sleep. He wants, perhaps, to discuss why a foolish lad won't let his friends protect him, or why he skips meals."

Lydia relaxed back. "Melinda?"

"Yes."

"Who else knows... about me?"

Melinda considered this. "Sean probably does. He's very observant, and he did carry you here. He wouldn't say a word about it, though. Or anything else," she added. "I can't tell you what Maisry knows. For all her chatter, she never tells anything that she considers to be secret."

"The king?"

Melinda cocked her head to one side. "No. The king sees a lot of things, but he hasn't *looked* at the minstrel." She paused, considering. "And sometimes a first impression is very hard to overcome, though I wouldn't count on that to protect you, lad." She tucked the blankets in and went back to the hearth, becoming a blurry shadow as Lydia's eyelids grew too heavy for her to keep open.

Despite the headache and the questions still whirling in her brain, Lydia drifted off to sleep.

*   *   *

Sunlight streamed in through the opened shutters, turning the polished furniture to ruddy gold. William sat fidgeting at some unease about the coming interview. He wasn't sure why. Certainly, none of his peers would have understood. *Alan is a servant*, they would have said.

None of his peers, however, were truly his peers. Raised as an only child, it was not as though he could turn to the children of other nobles for company. And once Melinda had gotten hold of his education, well... it might surprise several of his advisors how egalitarian his views truly were. So he wondered about the minstrel, and worried that he had not done right by him, whether servant or not.

It had been an impulse that had brought the lad to the castle, William knew. A momentary whim; if it had gone another way he might have left the lad on the doorstep, with a coin, perhaps. But he'd played the harp in a way that William had never thought to hear again and he'd let his heart dictate his actions.

Once he'd done that, though, he'd left the lad to others, not even giving him as much thought as a stray dog. He'd let others instruct him, and merely listened to the music, the beautiful music that reminded him of *her*.

He could still feel the shock of what Melinda had told him, of the bruises upon bruises that told of casual torment. In *his* palace. The minstrel had never said a word.

"He wouldn't," Melinda had said. "And if he keeps this up, he'll cut his own heart to ribbons." She'd looked at him with her hands on her hips. "He's yours, you know. Blood and bone. I don't know what you've done to deserve it."

Now he wondered what she had meant, and how she had known. To his certain knowledge, she'd never seen the two of them in the same room.

When the page brought Alan in, he could see the minstrel wasn't limping, though he was slow and placed his steps carefully. William indicated that he should sit down, and he sat in the chair straight-backed, looking at the floor.

William frowned in thought. The youth looked different somehow, not only from the purple and yellowing bruises that surrounded one eye. His brownish hair was cleaner than the king had ever seen it. It was almost a different color entirely, and was pulled behind his ears instead of falling to conceal his face. Perhaps that was it.

The tension was evident in the minstrel's posture, as though Alan waited for a worse blow than the ones the Baronet had given him. He'd hate to think he was the cause of that.

William straightened up, then said quietly, "I feel as though I've failed you."

"*Failed* me, majesty?" replied the minstrel, looking up in shock. William blinked; there was something odd about Alan's eyes. He continued, "I gave you a position and you were hurt under my own roof. I didn't protect you as I should."

"You saved my life," was the soft answer.

"The guards—" William began, and was interrupted.

"–Not then, sire. Before. When you brought me in."

The king thought back to the near skeletal youth, all but barefoot in the ice-rimmed cold, and realized how, even thin as he was, the youth before him was a picture of health next to that memory. "Why did you not tell anyone that the Baronet was beating you?"

The minstrel bit his lip. "Tell who?" he whispered.

"Someone. Anyone. Did you think you deserved to be beaten?" An idea occurred to him. "Did they beat the servants in your father's house?"

Alan's eyes flew wide, and then he jerked his gaze down to the floor. William amended his statement quietly. "Did they beat servants where you came from?"

The minstrel closed his eyes and whispered, "Yes."

And did you beat the servants, then, and consider your bruises a form of justice? William wondered, but did not voice. Orrin had said that Alan had the sort of training that only a noble could have received; a noble, or a page in the king's own castle. Whatever had driven him from his home, it was enough to have him deny his heritage. Somehow, William did not think it was pride. "Servants are not to be beaten, here. I know that is the common practice, but it is not fit for the keep of the king." He leaned forward, "And you are not a servant, anyway. You are a minstrel." Alan held on to the edge of the chair and continued to stare at the floor. "You don't know what that means, do you?" he added, curiously. Surely there had been minstrels at his father's keep, or how would he have learned the harp?

"No, your majesty," Alan replied as he realized that the king expected an answer. "I don't think I do."

William took a deep breath. " 'A minstrel is to be treated with respect, as music binds us together. None may beat him aside from his master, or at his master's behest, and then only for great offense. A minstrel is one who may speak without fear, lest we forget essential truths, and none may threaten to stop his tongue.' " Alan looked confused at the formal-sounding oration. "It's in the Charter, lad," added William.

"I did not know," came the reply.

"There's more," said the king, "about the specific duties of a minstrel, and the punishments for harming one. But the important part is that you are not a servant."

"Merely a minstrel without an instrument."

William grinned. "Your new harp should be arriving in a day or so."

He was pleased to see the minstrel's face light up. "A new harp?" It was the first hint of enthusiasm he had ever seen the youth display. William leaned back in his chair. "Baronet Roland bought it as part of his punishment. The rest of the fine will be added to your wages." William grew expansive. "We had to send all the way to Galeskeep for the harp."

The minstrel froze. "Galeskeep?" His happy look faded. "*How long was I ill?*"

William cursed himself. Melinda hadn't told Alan, and he, like a fool, had blurted it out. "You were unconscious for two days," he said. "You were feverish for four more." He looked once more at the minstrel's fading bruises. "Melinda wasn't sure you would live."

Alan turned his face aside, closed his eyes, and covered his mouth as if to hold in words he would regret. After a long moment, he inhaled sharply and took the hand away, saying to the wall, "And what would be done, sire, had I died?"

William had a sudden sense of reliving the past. He'd been there when Richard—he still couldn't think of him without sorrow—had received word of his twin sister's death. And he had done nothing, lost in his own grief.

He wouldn't make that mistake again.

"If you were a noble," William said finally, knowing that he might only be twisting the knife, "when you died, the crown could make an inquiry into your death. It is an obscure law, almost never used—such an inquiry is not solely meant to find out the truths behind a death, but to make life hard for the nobility involved. Anything is relevant in such an inquiry—taxes and tithes withheld, bribery, even secret mistresses. It is a punishment of sorts."

"But for a minstrel?" Alan pursued. As though it were all he was.

"For a minstrel," William said slowly, "there are bigger fines. Exile from court—for a time. Loss of custom. And he would have found it hard to hold a ball, as most musicians would avoid him. Most, I said.

He might well find some."

For a moment, William thought the youth might cry. Then Alan let out a ragged breath, and almost forced composure on his features. "So," he said, and stopped. In the long pause, William decided that, while they were on such uncomfortable topics, he might as well continue.

"Did you know the Lady Lydia?" he asked.

An indescribable look passed across the minstrel's face, of which astonishment played no small part. "A—After a fashion," he stammered. Strangely enough, this seemed to be a less painful topic. "We... had the same harp teacher."

"What was she like?" continued the king.

Alan pressed his lips together and sat up a little straighter. " Naïve. Romantic. Easily led," he said, a little bitterly. He looked just over William's shoulder. "The words," he added, "are those of Richard Kentwell."

"Her *brother?*" William replied, stunned. "I thought he loved her."

Still not quite meeting the king's eyes, Alan went on. "He did. He... thought her virtuous, good, and... deluded as to what the world was." His lips twisted. "And she was a pawn."

A pawn?" William whispered. The youth's evident pain was cutting. William was not often allowed to exercise his compassion, though he felt it keenly when he saw someone in pain. He had thought that the bullying was the cause of the pain he'd seen, but it appeared the cause lay elsewhere. If he could but draw Alan out...

The minstrel's bleak expression barely wavered as he said, "Lydia was everything you ever wanted, was she not?" At the king's tense nod, he continued, "It is only natural. She was raised that way. She was fed a steady diet of fireside tales, taught grace and manners and music..."

William shook his head. "I do not see it. It would not be the first time a family has done such..."

"*No*, your majesty," the minstrel interrupted. " Lady Lydia was to be a bride to tie the northlands tighter. The old Duke made the plan. Shape the daughter. Teach the son. Lure in the heir, then marry them off... and take over. Once she'd had a child or two, well… accidents happen, and who better to be regents?"

William shook his head. "That's insane. To risk so much, over so many years, on such a slim chance..."

"Slim?" Alan asked. "Where are your brothers, your majesty? Where are your cousins?" William was silent; the minstrel just shook his head. "The line of succession is not clear, your majesty. Your family is small and they saw opportunity."

"This hurts you," the king said after a moment. In truth, he found it difficult to imagine that this complicated plot could have come to fruition. But this youth acted as though this were the death of all his dreams.

"*Hurts* me? I..." Alan's voice cracked and he stopped. He sighed, and his shoulders slumped. "I played for the traitor at the king's command, and in a few short hours he divested me of a number of illusions. I suppose you could call it hurt."

"Did he recognize you?"

Alan blinked. "No reason he should, your majesty," he said, a little calmer. "He never knew me." The latter phrase had a peculiar emphasis, but sounded like the truth.

"Lydia... knew nothing of this, then?" William asked.

Alan sighed. "The Lady Lydia would rather have died than betray her king." Once again, he turned to look at the wall. "Do you know what he told me, majesty?"

Wide-eyed, William shook his head.

"He told me... that he was glad to die. That even as he rebelled, he didn't care if he succeeded, because he had not felt it when his twin sister died. He told me that he knew then, that he was beyond feeling." William barely heard the muttered afterthought, "The fool."

The king looked at the minstrel,tense in his chair, as though he were brooding. He asked, quietly, "Do you think the Lady Lydia loved me?"

Alan finally looked at him, and said in consideration, "She might have, your majesty. But had she known what her father and brother planned, she would have pretended to hate you, rather than draw you into their snare. She was, after all, raised to be loyal." His face was drawn and pale. William stood, and the minstrel looked up, alarmed.

William put one finger beneath the minstrel's chin and tilted his face up. Alan's eyes were wide, and the bruises mottled around the left one. William examined that gaze carefully and finally realized where the strangeness lay. Alan's left pupil was entirely dilated, injured perhaps when the Baronet hit him. He shook his head when the minstrel tried to get to his feet, and William went to the door. He spoke with the page for a moment, closed the door, and returned to his seat.

"You need food, Alan," he said. When the minstrel started to voice a denial, the king crossed his arms and put what he considered to be his most royal face on; it was the face his father had used when he was a small boy, refusing to listen to his tutors. The youth subsided. "You pretend to need nothing, but you can't live like that. What did I say about minstrels?"

Tension left the minstrel abruptly. " 'A minstrel is one who may speak without fear, lest we forget essential truths.' "

William raised his eyebrows. "You have a good memory." Orrin, in fact, had used the word "peerless," but he'd cautioned against telling the minstrel so. He suddenly wondered how old Alan was. Melinda called him "lad" but that might have been her own private joke. And surely someone as young as Alan appeared to be, could not be so incredibly complicated. "I should like your advice."

"*My* advice, majesty?" Alan asked, shaking his head slightly. "Why?"

"Because you're honest," William replied, and the minstrel's face fell.

"I cannot lie to you. I *cannot*. But..." He sighed and subsided.

Oddly enough, William guessed the cause. "I won't often ask you of things that pain you. The idea is to ask you of things that pain *me*. I need someone who will tell me the things I need to hear."

Color came back into Alan's cheeks. "Is this what a minstrel does?" he asked.

"Sometimes," came the reply.

The minstrel nodded, once. "I will do it, sire."

"William," the king corrected.

"What?"

"If you are to advise me," said the king, "without fear and without falsehood, you should use my name, not my title."

Alan squeezed his eyes shut, not in fear but as though the world had turned upside down, and that by concentrating hard, he could make it come right again. "I will do it... William."

"Was that so hard?"

Alan looked at him slantwise, a look that said both *Yes* and *No*. It rather cheered William.

There was a knock at the door, and the page entered, bearing a tray with a large bowl of stew. He placed it upon a small table to the minstrel's left. Bowing to the king, he said, "As you requested, your majesty, some food for the minstrel."

Alan was eyeing the stew with some trepidation. It was a very large bowl, almost a tureen. The page caught William's eye, and the king grinned. The page addressed the minstrel. "Melinda sends her compliments, and says you are to eat it all."

The look of dismay on Alan's face was almost comic. "*All* of it?" The page, stifling laughter, nodded. William crossed his arms and leaned back in his chair. With a bow to the king, the page left... but Alan had to finish his stew under the laughing gaze of the king.

*   *   *

Lydia was trembling as she left the study. She forced herself to go to her room, the room she had not been in for a week or more, if what the king had said were correct. She very carefully did not think of him as William. She closed the door carefully and realized she was shaking from the strain of telling that story.

She *had* turned it into a story, she realized, polishing the phrases in her mind, hoping that somehow phrasing it like a tale—or a history—would give her the distance she needed to bear it. She could hear Richard's voice in her head, clear as the night sky, telling her his sins and his dreams. His voice had been lifeless, as though all music had drained from his life. And Lydia had—at first—fought the impulse to reveal herself to him.

But as he continued, she no longer had to fight; In fact, she had begun to fear that he might somehow realize the truth of her deception. That he might realize just how cruel life had been to him.

Or how cruel he had been to her.

She'd spent a fortnight doing nothing but thinking—no, brooding—over that night. Now as the bottled emotion was finally released, she was surprised to discover what it was.

It was anger. Pure, unadulterated rage.

It gathered behind her eyes, throbbing in her bruises. She had never been so mad in her life, and was a little appalled at its strength. Her eyes lit on the tapestry across from her bed, at its colors of green and gold. The colors of Kentwell.

The colors of Richard.

Two steps were enough to bring her to the hanging and she grabbed at it and pulled. It resisted; she looked up long enough to see how the bar set, then a flip and a tug brought the whole assembly down in a cloud of dust. The plastered stone beneath was paler than the surrounding wall, streaked with cobwebs and water stains. She turned, knelt on the bed, and pulled down the hanging of the opposite wall.

The fury heated her more than an oven. She stripped off her tabard, glad that the linen shirt still came down low on her thighs. Pulling down the tapestries hadn't helped. Her eyes lit on the table, empty of harp or any other item. She missed her harp, ached for it, dimly aware that not even playing out her fury might be enough, but longing for the surcease all the same.

She grabbed her pillow and threw it, hard, at the wall; one of the unlit candles was knocked from its sconce. She walked over to the pillow, picked it up, and threw it again; this might almost do. She refused to scream, but in her mind she shrieked curses to the sky, damning Richard, damning the Baronet, and yes, damning the king. She'd feared being unmasked. She'd feared what would become of her, sister to a known traitor.

And she was utterly enraged that he hadn't recognized her at all.

She kept at it as the sun moved off the windows and the room dimmed. Her arm was getting sore from the unfamiliar repetition, but she didn't know what she'd do if she stopped. And then the door opened in the middle of her throw and the pillow caught Maisry right in the face.

Lydia collapsed down on the chest as though she'd been the one hit, her anger draining away. As Maisry blinked and looked around the disheveled room, Lydia began to shake. Her head throbbed, and she started to see little flashes of light. With a low moan, she curled up into a ball on the chest. Maisry rushed to her side.

It was Maisry who moved the tapestry off the bed, who retrieved the pillow from the doorway, and who had providentially brought a healing draught from Melinda—which she had managed to keep from spilling despite extreme provocation. It was Maisry who coaxed the minstrel onto the bed and carefully soothed her while she shuddered from the aftermath of her rage. But Lydia would not cry.

She lay on the bed, worn out, as Maisry put the room to rights... without hanging the tapestries, true, but she did restore the candles. When she had done that, Maisry looked around the room and said, quietly, "If you promise me that you will stop pretending to be a pell, I can show you to the practice yard, so that the next time you feel as though you need to hit something, it will be something that is meant to be hit."

Lydia cracked open her eyes. "A pell?"

Maisry said, gravely, "A pell is what the guardsmen use for a target when they are learning weaponry."

Strange that she could still call up a smile, Lydia said, "I have already tried being that. It does not work so well."

Maisry sat down on the edge of the bed. "No. That is why I want you to promise." She seemed serious.

Lydia drew in a shuddering breath and said, "I promise."

*   *   *

Dinner that night was an exercise in patience for Lydia. She found the solicitousness somehow annoying. The cooks fussed over her, the servers fussed over her—even the pages fussed over her. Lydia bore in mind that her flare of temper had left her with a raging headache, and that her mood was definitely soured thereby.

Lydia held her tongue until the third person asked if those far too visible bruises still hurt, and irritation spilled forth. "Yes, they still hurt, and yes, I have had enough to eat, and no, I don't need to sit closer to the fire!" she snapped. "I am not some fragile thing that must be treated carefully lest it break, not... some gently-born pampered lady who must be cozened and cosseted and kept safe from all harm!"

Her eyes stung—from the smoke, she told herself firmly. *I am not what they made me to be.*

A silence followed her remark, and Lydia was suddenly horrified. "I'm—I'm sorry," she stammered, "I didn't mean..."

One of the servers giggled, and Paige said, wryly, "Blows to the head usually loosen the brains, not the tongue." She smiled, then, and waved the others back about their business.

The servers' hall gained a more normal tempo. It gradually occurred to Lydia that people had been worried about her. She couldn't recall the last time someone had worried about her.

Well.

That was it, wasn't it? Back at the keep, she *had* been one of those pampered ladies, yet no one seemed to mark her except when she was there. The Lady Siona spoke gently to her, and gave her advice, but never once sought her out. Her maids had fussed at her and barely spoke above a mumble.

Richard, it seemed, had had his own concerns. Lydia rubbed her fingers against her temples, gently along the bruised side.

It was a strange feeling, this being cared for. Lydia couldn't quite fathom what she had done to deserve it. She felt as though she hadn't spoken to more than a dozen people since arriving at the castle.

Yet here was Jankin, smiling at her; there was Paige, with her seemingly endless supply of honeyed rolls; Maisry with her quips and sympathetic remarks; Lindy with her wide-eyed solemnity. And Melinda cared, too... astonishing that one person in control of so very much should spend so much time worrying about a starveling girl in boy's clothing.

And the king...

The king had worried about her. Well... he'd worried about his minstrel boy that he'd taken off the streets, but that minstrel boy was her. And he'd asked for her opinion. *Without fear, and without falsehood.*

Without fear. That was a goal worth aspiring to. *I have been afraid for so long... afraid for my life, afraid for my virtue, afraid I should starve.* Lydia looked around the hall, noting how incredibly healthy the servers looked, how only the pages in the throes of adolescence looked thin and stretched. *The pages and me,* she thought wryly.

Lydia breathed in slowly. Now that she thought on it, there was little that could happen to her that was worse than what she had already faced. If she were unmasked, she would take what would come. There was a curious relief in this thought, that she could face any punishment with equanimity.

When Maisry appeared before her, grinning, Lydia's resolve wavered. Surely that grin meant some devilment. "You made me a promise," Maisry proclaimed, and Lydia heard a few suppressed giggles. *Without fear,* she reminded herself, and stood and followed the maid out of the room. Maisry's steps grew quicker until she was all but running through the halls. Lydia following breathlessly behind.

They arrived at the practice yard, which was mostly deserted at the dinner hour. Maisry ran right up to one man; a stocky, graying man of indeterminate years whose face was tanned like old leather. "If you please, Martin," she said, not in the least bit out of breath, "Minstrel Alan should spend some time in the yard." She indicated the panting Lydia, and with a smile and a wave, ran back as easily as she had run out.

Martin raised one thick eyebrow, and looked at Lydia's bruises. He folded his arms and said, "Well?"

Lydia swallowed. "Maisry said... I should use a pell, not be one." He grunted.

Then he strode over to her, looked her up and down much the same way that Melinda had, and grabbed her hand. He prodded her palm a bit, looked at her fingers, and pushed back her sleeve to examine her arm. Lydia winced; she hadn't been throwing the pillow with any knowledge of how to move, and her arm was already protesting its misuse.

Martin made another grunt and dropped her arm. "You'll not be doing any heavy work, at least not to start with. And we can't do anything as might damage your hands. I don't want you doing anything without clearing it through me first; we have a lot of dangerous things hereabouts and I don't want you hurting yourself through ignorance." Lydia nodded, slowly.

The guardsman looked at her thoughtfully. "What do you want, then?"

"What do *I* want?"

Martin nodded. "I know what Maisry wants, but why are you here?" He took in the utterly baffled look on Lydia's face and relented. "Think on it, minstrel. Tomorrow, I will start with you. Tonight, you may run. If it becomes too much, walk, but don't stop. If ever you need to work off some anger," (Lydia swallowed) "running is always safe." He stepped back and looked at her until, gulping, she stumbled into a shuffling run.

She barely made half the circuit of the practice yard before she had to drop to a walk. It hurt, but not in the way that her jolted bruises hurt. She lengthened her strides, feeling the stretch in her legs, and soon was back up to a run. Within one circuit, her throat was on fire and she was swallowing convulsively, but she kept on. Somehow, this was better than that horrible, throbbing anger.

After three circuits, Martin waved her over and showed her a few stretches. They were precisely the sorts of things that skirts would make impossible, Lydia realized. After she caught her breath, she asked Martin, "Why?"

"Why what, minstrel?"

"Why are you doing this?" *Why do you care?*

Martin smiled. "You're one of ours, minstrel, and we take care of our own."

Lydia left the yard, very thoughtful. She went up to the office across from the library, where she had not been since her encounter with the Baronet.

"Master Orrin? I'd like to borrow a copy of the Charter."

*   *   *

William found he was drumming his fingers on the carved arm of the chair. Five beats, then four: a pattern he'd used since childhood whenever he was fidgety. He flattened his hand against his leg, but that didn't calm the fidgets.

What was wrong with him? All he was going to do was to have a conversation, a morning talk that would in all likelihood become a regular occurrence. If Alan agreed, that is. Perhaps there was the difficulty.

You would think that dealing with a minstrel boy would be less nerve-wracking than wrangling with the ambassador of Erlein. Yet his fidgety fingers—drumming again already—told a different tale. Melinda said that Alan was his, but William was afraid he was going to ask more of him than he had a right to. There hadn't been a King's Minstrel for nearly a century. To his amazement, William had apparently stumbled over a person who had the potential to fill that role.

Somehow the stories had neglected to mention how distressing an honest advisor could be. Twice, Alan had addressed him as an equal. Twice, the words had cut to the bone. The only consolation of sorts was that Alan hadn't hurt him any more than he'd hurt himself. That thought was also distressing.

William seized on that and wondered about it. He came to the conclusion that Melinda was right, that Alan was indeed his. He was responsible for him. So perhaps he felt responsible for Alan's distress as well? It was something to consider.

Alan, when he appeared, was not moving with the stiff grace of the previous morning. The stiffness, if anything, was exaggerated, as though Alan's muscles had turned to stone overnight. Dark circles under both eyes set off the ring of yellow and purple around the left one. The contrast was so great that William blurted out, "You look pursued by fiends."

"As well as that?" Alan said, with no small irony. He sat in the chair opposite the king and regarded him steadily. Then he said, with great deliberateness, "I have been reading the Charter."

William sat a little straighter in his chair. The minstrel continued, "I do not know who it was that wrote the duties of the Royal Minstrel down, but he spent very little time on the... musical aspects of the job. It seems that a minstrel is there to advise, to speak with visiting lords and ladies, their servants, and to find out all of their needs and concerns. He does not come out and say it, but it is obvious what he was most concerned with."

William nodded. "Information," he stated.

Alan looked at him strangely. "Truly, the emphasis is a little less on just listening and more on what might better be termed spying."

"Spying," William said, with disgust.

"If you do not like the word, do not encourage the action," the minstrel replied mildly. "I would prefer to merely observe, myself."

After a moment, the king nodded. This was, after all, what he had asked the previous day. "You take to honesty well," he said.

Alan waved that aside. "I would like to ask something, your majesty."

"William."

"*William*. I want to know … why me? What is it about me that makes you trust me with this? ...With anything, really? I am just a... a brothel-born guttersnipe."

William sat back and thought about this for a moment. The minstrel radiated a certain tension. The king hadn't missed the epithet, said in a speculative tone, not one that cut to the heart. No base-born youth would drop into this role with such ease. William put the thought of Melinda firmly out of his mind.

"There have been many minstrels that were only musicians," he began, finally. "They had all of the privileges and protections of Royal Minstrels, but never knew there was more to the position."

"How could they not?" asked Alan. "It is right there. It might not be obvious, but anyone with half a mind..."

"Most minstrels cannot read," said William, gently. Alan closed his mouth and looked thoughtful. "Of those who can read, only a handful would think to inquire about their duties, and most of those would interpret the text to mean that they should merely flatter and fawn, and to smooth the way for any decisions of the monarch." Alan looked at his hands, clenched in his lap. "It is a rare thing to have the honesty and intelligence needed for a Royal Minstrel paired with the musical abilities that the... more mundane aspects of the task require."

"But you trusted me yesterday," Alan persisted.

"I did," the king answered. "I do. I am not sure why. Perhaps it is that you are the first person—aside from Melinda—who seems concerned about me, and not my position."

Alan's eyes widened. "Oh no," he said. "I am very concerned with your position, *your majesty.* Primarily that you remain in it."

"Most people do not care who is king, as long as there is a king." He added, "And many of them would like to see themselves in such a position."

Alan curled a hand under his chin, the thumb resting against his lips. Then he folded his arms and said, "You are a new king, and there has already been rebellion. If you are seen as weak, then more will follow. They will be watching you closely."

"Who will?" William asked, intent.

Alan looked at him. "Those that pushed Kentwell into rebellion, sire."

The king gaped. "I thought Richard acted alone," he said. Perhaps it had been naïve of him to believe that.

"In a rebellion, does anyone truly act alone? I do not think that Kentwell had quite that level of initiative." The minstrel shrugged. "How did the Lady Lydia die?"

William had to think hard, for a moment; then he had it. "She was thrown from her horse on a ride."

"It was a horse that Richard Kentwell had purchased for her, had sent her as a gift. He blamed himself for her death." Alan shifted in his seat. "I find it convenient, your majesty, that her death should occur in such a fashion."

This line of reasoning was something that the king had not considered. "Are you sure of this?" he asked carefully.

The minstrel nodded. "I think that the lady's death was part of a larger plan, and that the young Duke was meant to fail."

"For what cause?" whispered the king.

Alan slumped. "I don't know, your majesty." His mouth twisted. "I don't know enough yet. I have no proof. Even a strong king requires proof, lest he be thought a tyrant."

"William."

"What?"

"William. You agreed to use my name."

"*William.* Why are you so insistent upon that?"

"And why are you so stubborn as to forget it? I do not think you forget things easily. Is this some message?"

"If it is a message, then you should not ignore it. Your majesty." He leaned back in his chair, wincing a bit. "You could call me Minstrel Alan, when it pleases you. To remind me of my place."

"Your place..." William trailed off. "You were made for this, I am sure." To be so at ease, with so little effort... and yet, to seem as though he belonged. Melinda had reported how the servants had taken to the lad as well. Someone who could move amongst the nobility and the servants alike was truly rare.

He wouldn't tell the minstrel that Melinda gathered information for him, though anyone with 'half a mind' would guess. A king needed more than one spy... and he suspected that Melinda only told him as much as she thought would do him good.

"It is as well," mused the minstrel. "A Royal Minstrel is one for life." The thought seemed to trouble him, but he visibly shook it off.

"So then, *Minstrel* Alan, what would you have a new king on an uncertain throne do to be seen as less weak?"

"Marry," replied the minstrel curtly.

William threw up his hands in frustration just as a knock came at the door and a page entered, bearing a tray piled with bread and cheese. This tray was placed on a table near the minstrel, who started, then glared at the king. "Is this going to be a regular occurrence?" Turning to the page, he said, "At least bring something for the king. This is absurd."

The page bowed, hiding a smile, and left. Alan tore off a piece of bread and broke off a bit of cheese, shrugged, and started to eat. The king said, "Melinda looks out for your welfare."

"In the most public way possible. I think she is convinced that I will starve myself if given the chance."

"Were you not?" William asked.

"I was distracted. I am no longer." He glared at the bread, and said in a softer tone, "Sooner or later, you forget to be hungry." Alan leaned forward. "We were speaking of your marriage."

"You say that as though it were the easiest thing in the world to arrange."

"For a king, it is not, true. But it is necessary." The minstrel tore off another piece of bread and shook it at the king. "For alliances, for land, and for heirs, a king must be married."

"What of love?"

Alan sighed. "What has love to do with marriage when it comes to kings?" He absent-mindedly began to roll the bread between his fingers. "I fear it is my place to tell you the unpleasant truths. If you do not choose a wife, and soon, either one will be chosen for you, or your heir will choose himself." He bit his lip. "Marrying for l-love would have signaled your death." He looked down at the smashed bread in his hand and carefully placed it back on the tray. The he rubbed at his temple, saying, "Forgive me, ma-William. I—" He trailed off, and stood, gingerly.

The king stood as well, but Alan waved him off, drew himself up with some small effort, and gave a very creditable bow. "With your permission?" he asked. William nodded. He'd forgotten, in the conversation, that the minstrel was barely healed from the beating. He rather suspected that Alan had as well.

*   *   *

Lydia went to her room, and considered lying down. Then, she shook her head and pulled the livery off, changing into the shirt, tunic, and simple trows that she'd been given when she had first arrived. *What do I want? I want not to think.*

Her strides were long, pulling against stiff muscles. She refused to give in. Some part of her protested that it wasn't fair, but she suppressed it.

Fair? Was it fair for girls who were years younger than her to be used in a brothel? Was it fair for brigands with lovely low voices and stolen clothes to assault travelers on the roadside, leaving scavenged corpses and lonely hearths?

Was it fair that she should have had so much, and nothing at all?

There were so many things she could do nothing about. Well, there were still things that she could change.

She found the practice yard filled with guards doing various exercises. Martin was nowhere to be seen. As he had suggested, she broke into a slow trot.

One foot in front of the other. She began to count the steps in her head, trying to blot out her ever-circling thoughts. When that didn't work, she used the rhythm of her footsteps as the beat, and mentally sang ballads. Soon, she was gasping for breath, but she didn't slow down; her muscles screamed at her, but she wouldn't slow down.

She finally collapsed against the wall, gasping, almost sobbing. She couldn't move. And her stomach was cramping, though that was a familiar sensation and could be fought off.

Hands on her shoulders helped her stand and guided her, still wheezing, in the direction of a tall, freestanding pump. She closed her eyes and bent over, hands on her knees, as a wave of astonishingly cold water slammed onto her head. She staggered over to a pile of padding and fell onto it, rolling over to see Martin, hands on his hips, standing over her. "Not good," he said, "not good at all."

Lydia wheezed up at him. Suddenly, not thinking was very easy. At least the look on Martin's face was concerned rather than angry. He shook his head. "You trying to kill yourself, lad?" Lydia shook her head. "You pushed yourself too hard, minstrel. A little at a time is well enough. What do you want?"

Raggedly, Lydia replied, "I want..." It was hard, this thinking in terms of what she wanted. It wasn't a question she'd encountered before. She finally looked Martin straight in the eyes and said, "I want to never go through a beating again."

Martin nodded. "That's a good goal. But you mustn't pound *yourself* into the ground in doing it." He looked at her, sprawled and dripping. "I've a mind to start you on archery, but not today. Water's no good for the bowstring. Go and rest, minstrel. You can't do everything in one day."

He had to help her stand. Her legs didn't want to support her.

*   *   *

She fell asleep in the bath, later, and woke with a start in cold water. Adrenaline lent her strength and she was toweled dry and back in her room before her mind had caught up with her body. She struggled into her livery, wondering how late she was, and it was only when she reached for her absent harp that she realized that she wouldn't be playing at dinner that evening.

She sank down on the chest and rested her chin in her palms. Then she stretched her hands out in front of her, bending further and further until her cheeks were resting on her knees. Naturally, that's when Maisry chose to enter. She eyed Lydia with some amusement. "What are you, some sort of rag doll?"

"I feel like one," Lydia replied. "Haven't you heard of knocking?"

Maisry quirked her eyebrows. "Maids don't knock. We enter, do our jobs, and leave quietly. Or not so quietly, if our job is to drag a reluctant minstrel down to dinner. Aren't you hungry?"

Lydia mumbled, "Not reluctant. Tired." Maisry had already grabbed her hand and was dragging her upright. "I *heard*; in trying to outrun yourself. That's almost as bad as tearing your room to pieces."

"I wasn't..." Lydia started. Maybe she was. "River, oh river, carry my troubles away," she said softly.

Maisry nodded, and sang the next line. "*My love has proved false; she is bound to another; oh river, dear river, help me as you may.* Which I dearly hope you're not considering," she added.

"No," Lydia said, and smiled. "You have a nice voice."

"Thank you, minstrel," replied the maid.

*   *   *

The archery lesson turned out to be rather different than Lydia had expected. The first thing that the yardmaster did was to sit her down and treat her to a long lecture about examining the bow, arrows, and string for flaws. He handed her an arrow, and pointed out the long crack in the shaft, all but invisible until the arrow was flexed. "You shoot that, and you could end up with an arm full of splinters. Or it could be your face."

He told her about dry-firing, when one releases the string without an arrow on it, and warned her of dire consequences if he ever caught her doing it. "The worst part is that I don't do anything to you directly.

You just get to fire that same bow ten or fifteen times, to see if it's damaged. You'll know if it's damaged when it breaks."

Then he handed her a brace for her arm, and a leather tab for her fingers. Then he drew a line in the dirt. "Put your toes on that line," he said, "Now draw back on the string". Mindful of the prohibition against dry-firing, Lydia looked a question, to which he replied, "Just don't release it, that's all."

She nodded and wrapped her fingers around the string, pulling back. Then she held, which was incredibly difficult, while Martin walked around her and corrected her stance. "Rotate your arm a bit... drop that elbow... hold your thumb along your jawline. If you do it the same way every time, your aim will be better." He finally allowed her to relax the string. Then he had her practice her draw again, and again, until her arms felt as bad as her legs. Finally, he grunted, and led her through a small gate to a target yard that she hadn't even known existed.

Martin gave her a handful of arrows and showed her how to rest them in the ground quiver. She looked at each one carefully, which earned her a grin, and held the bow out in her left hand, an arrow in her right. "Turn your hand so it's palm down," he said. Then he rested the arrow on top of the sideways bow, showing her how the colored feather stood up, positioned so it wouldn't tear itself off on the bow. "Now right the bow, draw, and aim. Take your time; speed comes with practice. You should release by simply straightening your fingers."

Lydia sighted down the arrow, lining the tip right up with the bull's blot. She turned her elbow out, calmed her breath, and released the arrow. The string smacked against the brace with incredible force, and almost tore it off. The arrow stuck into the target low and to the left. "Aim a little higher," Martin said. "When you have a stronger pull, I'll teach you about undershooting your target." Lydia did as she was told, turning her elbow out just before she released. When she didn't, the brace threatened to go flying. She'd have a welt there before long.

None of her arrows came anywhere near the blot, though she lined them up every time.

When she had shot a dozen arrows, Martin walked with her to the target, the left side of which was bristling. The yardmaster looked at it, and muttered, "I should have thought of that earlier. Minstrel, hold your arms out and make a small circle with your hands." Lydia placed the bow on her feet and did so. "Now look at me through it," he said. Bewildered, she did.

"I wouldn't have guessed," Martin said. "You aim with your left eye. That's unusual for a right hander. We'll start you over, with your left hand this time."

That was distinctly harder. The arrow wavered away from the bow as she drew, and she felt distinctly clumsy. Her arm started trembling after only a few draws, and Martin called it a day. Lydia asked what he meant by aiming with her left eye.

"Ah. Well, have you ever closed one eye, then the other, and seen everything jump? One of your eyes sets the aim, so to speak." He looked at her. "Usually it's the same as the hand you use, though I've come across a few odds. It's strange, though, that yours should be the one that's damaged."

Lydia felt the same crawling fear she'd felt when the king had told her she'd almost died. "Damaged?"

Martin's face fell. "Ah. Sorry. It's just the pupil, you see. You were punched in the face. Sometimes that happens."

Lydia closed one eye, then the other. The world did seem to jump a bit. And the view from her left eye was just the tiniest bit washed-out. Then she shrugged.

*   *   *

The new harp was a thing of beauty. William admired its graceful curves and delicate inlays, and turned it a bit so that the muted sunlight fell on it to best advantage. That was silly, he knew, but it really did feel as though he were giving a gift of his own, rather than passing along a forfeit.

When Alan entered the room, his quick inhalation of breath gratified the king. He visibly restrained himself until William waved a hand towards it. He all but ran over to look at it. A moment's look sufficed to locate the case, and the key.The minstrel began happily tuning the strings, all but ignoring the other person in the room.

He was even humming a bit, quietly. William suddenly realized he was tuning to the hum, and turned to get a small package of his own. "Here. Use this," he said, and extended a small pouch.

Alan looked, up, puzzled, and drew out a tuning fork. His smile was sudden and dazzling, and he slapped the fork across the heel of his hand and looked around. Placing it against the table hardly did anything; it was too solidly made. Then he placed it against the harp's soundbox and one pure note filled the room. William blinked.

The note had barely begun to fade when the minstrel motioned him over. "Look," was all he said, as he set the fork humming again. When he placed it against the soundbox, three distinct strings began to vibrate, about one octave apart.

"They're in tune," William breathed, fascinated.

Alan nodded. "Of course they are," he said, and twisted the last knobs. The whole process had taken no more than a few minutes.

Alan sighed happily and laid his cheek against the polished wood. "I am very glad that this came, sire. It is hard to be without music." He strummed the strings gently and their pure tone shimmered off the walls. Then, he gathered up the harp and sat on a footstool with it in his lap.

The tune he played was slow, and lamenting. After a moment, the king fitted words to the melody. *River of sorrows, river of grace. Sweet gentle water to cover my grief...* he interrupted the song. "What's wrong, Alan?"

The minstrel looked up at him in some surprise. "Wrong? ... Oh! The song. Something brought it to mind." He smiled a bit apologetically. "It is a pretty melody."

William considered this. For him, the music and lyrics were as one, but for the harpist—the harpist who never sang, he realized—the melody could be all. "You could play 'Shall I Come to Thee.' Or," he grinned, " 'Rosemary, Thistle, and Thorn.' "

Alan made a face. "I suppose I deserved that," he said. "It has always seemed absurd to me that someone should string their harp with the hair of a dead girl. For one thing, hair would break in a few moments."

William sobered. "What made you do it, then?"

"I did not *string* the harp with the hair," he protested. "The old harp buzzed and grated. I needed to tack something in to soften it—I did not have access to the glues to mend it properly."

William nodded. "And where did you get that braid?"

"Have you made any plans to marry, sire?" the minstrel countered.

"You didn't answer my question."

"And you did not answer mine," Alan replied. "We must be even." Then he caught the king's eye and began to play "Shall I Come to Thee." William flushed as he realized that he had suggested a love song, which made the minstrel's argument rather pointedly. "Why won't you answer that question?"

"Which question?" the minstrel asked, still playing.

"How you came by the braid," William replied.

Alan shook his head. "My secrets are my own, and besides, the question is irrelevant. You mean to ask, 'Is it Lydia's braid', and 'how then did you come by it', and for that, I have no answer." It was a little unnerving to see his fingers continue so competently while his thoughts were elsewhere. "Or you mean to avoid the question of your marriage by speaking of love. William," he stopped playing, "she is dead."

"Or I could just be curious," the king muttered, and sank down in his chair.

The minstrel nodded composedly. "You could," he replied. "Yet even the servants know that you have not been the same since you received word of her death. You hired me because I played the harp as she did."

William stiffened. "I did not..." He broke off as the minstrel began playing again; it was the song he'd played on the street, but the music changed, becoming simpler, recognizable as "The Loathly Wyrm." Alan looked at him and said, gently, "Did you not?"

The song had been much in evidence on that visit, so long ago. William nodded curtly, an acknowledgment of the justice in the minstrel's charge. "You refuse to leave me any comfort in my memories, don't you?"

Alan stopped and rubbed his fingertips, looking at them a bit bemusedly. "I cannot think that they are comforting, if they have caused you so much pain this last year. You have built Lydia up into some untouchable saint or angel, and grieved her long. She was a real girl, and she died, and life continues for kings and for minstrels."

William stared at the lad. This attitude was completely different from the hurt anger of two days gone. It was as though the harp had changed the minstrel into a different person. "How can you be so calm?" he blurted out.

"I'm not," replied the minstrel serenely. "But I can pretend, and hope that seeming will become truth."

William wondered, but let it pass. "Will you play 'The Loathly Wyrm' at supper, then?"

Alan looked at the floor for a moment. "I meant to never play it again," he replied.

*   *   *

The minstrel slipped into the hall so quietly that night that the first indication that the diners had was a glissando of sound as he began to play. The new harp was a presence, where the old harp had been muted; William noticed absently that the songs were sprightly, even mocking.

The Erliena ambassador, who had arrived bare days previously, looked at the minstrel in some surprise. "I did not know, your majesty, that you had an instrumentalist of such skill," he said. William blinked as the song became unbelievably complicated for a minute, almost as though Alan had heard the low murmur. The man went on, "Our court would be most gratified to hire him when he has done with his contract."

"I do not intend to let him go," William replied. Jordeth of Guardron grunted. He'd thought it was foolish of William to make the lad a minstrel without a trial period. William hadn't bothered to explain the impulse, for impulse is what it truly was. He'd been luckier than he deserved.

"I see," said the ambassador smoothly. "Perhaps he might be a member of your ambassador's party, for a while."

"Perhaps," replied William, non-commital.

The lord of Guardron snorted. "He doesn't even sing," he muttered. "Says his voice is unsuitable."

Ambassador Liend raised one amber eyebrow. "Indeed?" He examined the minstrel, and a fleeting frown crossed his face as he noted the bruises and how sharply the harpist's cheekbones stood out. "I see," came the quiet murmur, and the king winced.

"Minstrel Alan is a recent addition to our court." William mentally cursed the presence of Jord at this table, this night. His blunt manners were normally a welcome respite from the fawning flattery of most of the court, but they were bound to come into friction with a polished diplomat's views. "He is in the hands of our most capable healer."

While the ambassador's expression did not change, the tension lightened somewhat. William looked over at the minstrel, a sudden thought making him frown. *Unsuitable voice?*

He'd tuned the harp to his hum.

He picked up his wineglass and turned back to the conversation. Ambassador Liend was a most observant man, and the king should not be seen to let his attention wander.

*   *   *

"You didn't bring your harp?" was the king's startled question the next morning. He'd have thought, from the minstrel's reaction the previous day, that the harp would accompany him everywhere.

Alan made a face as he sat on the upholstered footstool. "I did not play for... what, a fortnight?" He turned his hands up, showing off reddened fingertips. "I spent most of yesterday acquainting myself with the new strings. They're a bit stiffer than the old." The minstrel winced when the king took hold of his left hand.

William asked, "Did I hurt you?"

"Well... truthfully, yes," admitted the minstrel. "But between my bruises, my archery lessons, and overplaying my fingers, that should hardly surprise you." He bit his lip as the king turned his hand. The fingertips were red, though not blistering.

"Archery, then?" inquired the king.

"Yardmaster Martin thought it the best training. The string hits at a different point than harp strings." William let the minstrel's hand go. Alan flexed it once, twice, then stretched it until his palm turned white. He examined it thoughtfully, then lowered it to his lap.

William swallowed. "The ambassador asked me to convey his compliments." Alan looked up and tilted his head a fraction. "I know," he said with a hint of amusement in his voice. "He stopped me this morning and offered me a place in his staff."

The king's eyebrows shot up. "He did?" The minstrel nodded. "A place, two servants of my own, and," he added, grinning, "an income to 'support a wife.' "

"A wife?"

Alan nodded gravely, a sparkle in his eyes. "He thinks that I am treated badly, here. I was quiet, polite, and kept turning the talk to music. I believe I have him convinced I am half-mad for it."

William laughed. "That's one way to stop persistent offers," he said. The minstrel shook his head. "Erleina consider music sacred. Being half-mad for it might be a good thing."

The king blinked. Alan took note of the somewhat perplexed look sitting on William's face, and continued: "A good musician is worth much there. Ambassador Liend hopes to improve his consequence by... well... salvaging a good musician from us eastern barbarians."

"I had no idea," William ventured. Alan frowned. "You should; is that not what Master Orrin is for? Music for an Erleinai is sacred, a gift to the Lord." William nodded tentatively; one of the titles for the god was Lord of Song. "It is not just what we would consider sacred music—they call all music 'the Voice of God.' And those who can create it have the status of saints—or perhaps divine madmen would be a closer example."

This was a little strange to William's ears. He liked music, had—until this last year—sought it out, but the idea of music as more than that seemed theologically unsound. "What of the Lady?" he ventured.

"They call her the Dancer," Alan replied. William thought of a graceful lady in swaying skirts, but that image was interrupted as Alan went on, "She is usually depicted with swords."

"You are joking."

"I am not." The minstrel looked at him, considering. "You really do need to talk to Master Orrin, sire." He folded his hands carefully and turned his eyes down as he added, "Unless you wish to lose me to the ambassador and an unnamed Erleinai wife."

"You..." William spluttered. "You..." He trailed off. "How old are you?"

Alan lifted his eyes. A slight quirk of the lips might be amusement. "Nineteen, your majesty."

"*William,*" sighed that worthy.

"I am still nineteen," replied the minstrel, not at all contrite.

William studied Alan for a moment. "You hardly look it."

"I *look* like a starveling whipping boy," the minstrel replied with peculiar emphasis.

William looked at the splotchy yellowed bruises around the minstrel's left eye, then at the thin, straight nose that had never been broken, remembering teeth that were neat and even and well cared for. "Perhaps," he said. What the minstrel really looked like was a young nobleman who'd fallen off a horse. Admittedly, a young nobleman who had been lost in the woods with nothing to eat for a month, and years younger than the age he claimed, but not worse than that. He laughed suddenly and sat down.

"What is it?" asked the minstrel.

"You."

"I don't understand."

William didn't elaborate. Alan's sense of humor lightened his mood, though he wasn't entirely sure the minstrel was trying to be funny. The precise manner in which the minstrel treated him was slipping, ever so slightly, giving William hope that someday, the minstrel would forget to treat the king as a benefactor, and superior. Alan would make a good friend.

William needed a friend.

"What do you want, Alan?" he asked suddenly. The minstrel held absolutely still.

"Everyone keeps asking me that," he murmured. Then, louder, he said, "I want you to be happy, William."

William opened his mouth for a joking reply. Then he looked at the minstrel's face, which was dead serious. *Blood and bone.* "Well," he managed after a long moment, "that is hardly what you want, is it? Besides, if I am to be happy, I need a better example before me."

"I *am* happy." William stared at the minstrel. This solemn youngster — assertions of nineteen aside —

was happy? Alan blithely went on, "I'm the happiest I've ever been in my life." He looked straight at the king as the silence drew out. "What?"

"You're happy?"

"Well... yes." Then he flashed that sudden smile. "Bruised, and stiff, and with legs that feel ready to fall off, but happy, yes. Ask me tomorrow and that may change." A knock came at the door. "And there is our refreshment." He stood and walked over to the door, taking the entering page by the shoulder and steering him in front of the king. The tray this time held a selection of pastries, and the page—a youth with black hair and the promise of height in his lankiness—looked a little startled.

"Have you two met?" the minstrel asked. He continued, "Your majesty, this is Page Jankin. Page Jankin, this is King William." He took the tray of pastries so that the flushing page could bow. He whispered something in the page's ear, at which the page bowed again and started backing out of the room. "Be sure to tell Master Orrin that I have not forgotten him," Alan said just before the page left.

He placed the pastries on a table within reach of the king, then chose another footstool within easy reach, looking at the king with a lopsided smile. "You see, your majesty," he said, ignoring the quiet protest of *William*, "I am free now."

"Free for what?"

"Free of being another's pawn. Free to find out who I am."

Is that why he would not speak of his past? William wondered. Aloud, he said, "And who are you?"

"Alan, the King's Minstrel," he replied with relish.

"And what does Alan, King's Minstrel, want?" William persisted.

Alan cocked his head slightly. "I want to know," he said after a moment.

"You want to know what?"

"*Everything*," the minstrel breathed out. William had to laugh at the expression of greed that Alan feigned, and dropped the subject.

*   *   *

A black bird with red epaulets sat cheekily on the fence. It sang a liquid trill at Lydia, who whistled back as she ran her hands down the shafts of her arrows, one by one. She found flaws far more easily by this method. Suddenly startled, the bird flew off, and Lydia heard the yardmaster speak from behind her. "You're here early," he said mildly.

She turned and twisted her lips. "I should be studying up for Master Orrin," she replied, "but I just can't wrap my head around what he wants."

Martin smiled broadly. "You wouldn't be the first, laddie. What's he asked of you?"

She shrugged. "It's about the border wars, twenty or thirty years back." She thought a minute. "Twenty-six years, it would be. There was a battle up near Mithe Áne that just doesn't make any sense. I—I don't know quite how to phrase it, but the battle reports just seem odd."

The yardmaster's grin never wavered. "Perhaps you'd like to hear from someone who was there?" When Lydia raised her eyebrows, Martin gestured broadly at himself. She stared for a moment, then burst out laughing. "Did Master Orrin ask you to do this?"

Martin shook his head. "No, Minstrel, he did not." Then the grin was back. "I am sure he accounted for it, though."

Lydia sank down to the ground, cross-legged. "Tell on, good sir," she said, with an inviting wave of her arm. "What have I missed?"

"Scree," he replied, succinctly.

"Scree?" She echoed, confused.

"That battle, the one giving you fits; it took place on one of the black hills southeast of the mountain. I don't think anyone would have picked that place to fight if we'd had the choice. Those mountains are steep and covered in rocks and loose dirt. Horrible footing. It's called 'scree', perhaps because of the sound it makes as it falls."

Lydia couldn't decide how to take this. *A crazy battle report and all because of bad footing?* "I suppose... well, I am not a fighter. Was it truly bad?"

Martin no longer looked so cheerful. "You need to remember that where you are, where you stand, is vitally important to how you fight. If you swing and tumble with a sword in your hand... well, as I said, no one would have picked there to fight. We both withdrew eventually."

"Oh," was all she could think of to say. Martin studied her for a moment, then said, "I haven't seen you practicing your harp about much. Several of the sentries have mentioned your absence," he added wryly.

Lydia shrugged. "It's been foggy most days," she said. "I can't practice—for much the same reasons you don't let out the bows."

Martin studied her for a moment. "Then you should, perhaps, leave your rooms on those days. There will come a time when you will be in want of friends and it is hard to make friends with someone who is rarely seen." Ignoring her astonishment—and her sudden thoughtful look—he turned and left as silently as he had come.

The Merry Man and the Maid

A Master of Musick came with an intent,
To give me a lesson on my instrument,
I thank'd him for nothing, but bid him be gone,
For my little fiddle should not be plaid on.

> *My thing is my own, and I'll keep it so still*
> *Yet other young lasses may do as they will.*
> *My thing is my own, and I'll keep it so still*
> *Yet other young lasses may do as they will.*

"How will you dress for the festival?" asked Maisry one early summer morning.

"The festival?" returned Lydia, startled. She counted the days over in her mind and realized, with some shock, that she had been in the palace nearly four months. Maid's Day and Lady's Breath had passed by, which meant that this must be...

"The Festival of Folly," Maisry said, impatiently. "Melinda lets us go through the stores and dress as we will. Did you not dress up last year?"

Lydia smiled up easily from her perch on the bench under the windows. "Last year, I was portraying the role of a street musician, desperate for coin. The outfit was simple." Paige dumped an armful of greens in the basin next to her and began washing dirt away.

"We could dress you up as a girl," Maisry mused. "You're certainly pretty enough."

Lydia kept smiling, though she mentally winced. "If I'm pretty enough, it would hardly be folly to dress me as a girl, now would it?" An image of a tall young guard occurred to her. "You had better to dress *Sean* up as a girl."

Maisry flushed bright red as Paige went off into gales of laughter. Lydia, startled, smiled even wider after a moment. The mockingbird and the stone. What a thing to guess. Maisry said, tightly, "Sean is on duty for the festival. So that is that."

"You must admit the idea has merit."

"Well... yes," Maisry said, her flush easing. "But what of you? You can't go to the festival dressed in livery."

"Go to the festival?" asked Lydia. She hadn't even considered it.

"I believe you haven't set foot outside these walls since they brought you here," the maid flared. Lydia had to admit, ruefully, that Maisry had a point. She might be ever underfoot within the castle, but she hadn't gone through the gates even once since Sean had led her here. She spread her hands in acquiescence.

"I will look through the stores, I promise." She tilted her head a bit. "I think I shall go as a nobleman. Does Melinda have anything in blue and yellow?"

Maisry frowned at her. "Blue and...? Oh. Yes, I see." She put her hands on her hips. "I think I shall dress up as a noble*man* too. We could be a matched set."

"You will come with me?" Lydia seized on this offer quickly. A jaunt outside the castle was a little frightening. *Without fear*, she reminded herself sternly.

The maid nodded, slowly. "I think you need to be shown how to have fun."

"I already know how to be a fool," Lydia agreed.

*   *   *

A few days later, the two girls—disguised and doubly-disguised—ran out of the gates, nodding only briefly to the guards. Beneath Lydia's shirt clinked a pouch full of coin. She'd been mildly surprised to find out how much she had earned, in wages and gifts, when she had gone to the controller. Since she had no need for coin within the castle walls, she'd just let it pile up.

The pouch was a bit heavier than the cost of food alone. "The price of folly," she'd told the controller, who had nodded. There was still plenty enough left—Lord and Lady, there was almost enough for a second instrument! Lydia had decided to consider that idea later.

Maisry was resplendent in a purple doublet trimmed with white and yellow ribbon. Her slashed sleeves had faded to nearly lavender, but the outfit looked all the finer for the contrast. A huge floppy hat with pheasant feathers covered the braids pinned to her head. She skipped gleefully, occasioning admiring glances at her hose-clad legs.

Lydia had managed to find a doublet in the Chardon colors, but it was far too large for her. Instead, she was wearing a navy jacket over a light blue shirt, matching hose, and the puffed knee-length breeches of a decades-old fashion. The outfit was all of a piece but properly silly, she hoped. As they pelted through the streets, she smiled to think how well her sessions in the practice yard were paying off. She could now keep pace with the younger girl.

Lydia was still gaining weight, though slowly. But instead of the soft curves that she used to have, wiry muscle added to her disguise. It didn't hurt to be able to outrun attackers, she mused. Martin had also been instructing her in how to see a dangerous situation before it became overt, and how to break simple holds. Lydia hoped that she would have to use none of these techniques at the festival.

When Maisry pulled up short, Lydia did as well, noticing that she was hardly out of breath. The smell of fresh sweets hit her like a wave, and for once, it was Maisry who was the one being dragged. Two sticky pastries later, the girls sailed into the fray.

There were villagers dressed as animals with furry pelts over their heads. There were men dressed as women, and women dressed as children; there were fools aplenty in rags and tags and bright with ribbons.

There was an impromptu parade, with a peasant carried around on the shoulders of two men dressed as horses. Soon, Lydia was laughing so hard that her sides ached, and a nearby fool upbraided her for her solemnity.

She spent a copper on a game of skill. Her aim was appalling, no matter which hand she used. It did not seem quite as strange as she had thought, tossing balls with her left hand. The stacked tumblers remained untouched regardless.

She watched carefully as a man flipped a leather-wrapped stick with tassels on its ends between other sticks held in his hands. "It is folly for you to do so well," she cried, and took the offered toys from the juggler. Naturally, it was only a few moments before the knack escaped her and the sticks went flying. With a laugh, she returned the sticks and tossed him a coin. Maisry looked a little concerned; Lydia merely said, "It is my folly to waste my coins on street performers."

They joined a circle dance next, jumping wildly as the music pulled them this way and that. Lydia bought some mead, for both she and Maisry were getting very thirsty. Then she looked up, intrigued, and pulled Maisry out of the main flow of people, to a lute player sitting on a worn blanket. She stood and listened as he went through a song, nodding in approval. She crouched down and spoke in a low voice. Maisry saw a glint of silver, not copper, in the minstrel's hand; the coin was passed to the lutenist as Lydia stood and brushed her hands against her knees.

Maisry hissed at her as they walked away, "What were you doing?"

Lydia replied, "Telling her to get out of the city before too long, and giving her the coin to run."

"Her?"

"Her."

"How, by the Lady, did you know? She's dressed like a boy..."

"Maisry."

Maisry looked at herself. "I suppose I should have guessed, shouldn't I? It's not as though..."

"Maisry," Lydia said again.

The maid looked her, and smiled ruefully. "You don't have to say it," she said, when it looked as though Lydia was about to speak. "I know. But if you don't tell me, then I can pretend I don't."

Lydia goggled at her. Maisry continued, "I'm glad you decided to trust me with your secret."

"I'm not even sure that it *is* a secret anymore!" Lydia retorted.

Maisry looked at her solemnly. "You saw yourself in the lute player, didn't you?" Lydia nodded.

This was the flush time, when a street musician could earn much, but winter was hard, and she feared the lutenist would not get her happy ending.

The maid was still regarding her. "I think I have to ask who Alan was, though."

Lydia smiled. Her smiles came more easily now, practiced while listening to the castle-folk. "Alan was the name of the minstrel who taught me the harp," she replied. Then she giggled, without fear of exposure, and poked a finger at Maisry. "And *you*, you are too solemn! Allow me my folly and join me in it!" Maisry giggled in return. She laughed as she pulled Lydia back into the throng.

Soon, Lydia had found the festival stalls. Flush for the first time in her life, she was struck by the uncertainty of not knowing what to buy. She couldn't buy it all, nor did she want to, but she understood for the first time, the saying that 'money wished to fly away'.

One seller had basketfuls of ribbons, freshly dyed in saffron and madder and cobalt hues. Lydia looked at them wistfully, but had little reason to linger. Even foppish minstrels—and she hadn't exactly represented herself as such—did not need much in the way of ribbons.

Another stall showed off toys of gallant knights and jointed wooden horses, brave with paint and promise. She'd had a few such toys back at the keep. There was a fabric stall, and one selling thread. Lydia bit her lip in frustration.

Maisry noted the indecision, and took her by the arm, dragging her off toward the smell of freshly baked meats. "Food first," she insisted. "Then we can browse!"

Lydia bought them both spiced pasties, savory with spring onion. Simple though the dish was, the festival atmosphere made it into something special, a treat to remember. She sighed in complete happiness, licking her fingers, when Maisry dragged her to a wine stall to wet their throats. She bought a skin, realizing that she'd already dried her throat out once that day and it might be a while before they swung by another seller.

Maisry then spent some time bargaining at the ribbon-seller's for some embroidery thread. Lydia found a bookseller and thumbed thoughtfully through the offerings, but in the end came away with a wallet of paper. Storybooks just didn't seem as interesting as they had before. She tapped the wallet against her hand as she looked around the booths. Paper was just too... practical.

Then she spied the colorful clay whistles at a potter's booth. With a whoop of discovery, she grabbed Maisry and dodged her way over. She paused, staring intently. When the potter came over to bargain, she surprised Maisry by dealing to purchase two. Lydia then spent several minutes testing the various whistles until she found two that meshed well. She draped one cord over Maisry's head, bringing a smile from the potter.

"You two," he paused and grinned, "noble sirs, have fun now!"

Maisry protested as they walked away, "I can't play this!" Lydia shrugged. She knew that the real protest was that Maisry didn't have extra coin to sling around and felt that she couldn't return the favor.

After a moment's thought, Lydia said, "I can't play it either. But I know you can sing, so... I thought I'd get something you could play around on." She held up her own, a vibrant emerald, and ventured a few notes. Her fingers, so sure on the harp, got tangled, and the tune resolved into an undignified squeak. She looked at Maisry gravely, eyebrows raised brazenly, challenging her to imitation. After a moment, Maisry raised her own speckled blue whistle, and tried a few notes of her own.

After many false starts, they began to get the hang of the bulbous instruments, and played as best as they could through giggles. Then Maisry started playing "My Lady's Hairbrush" and Lydia all but inhaled her whistle. "Where did you learn *that?*" she asked, after she'd stopped choking.

Instead of answering, Maisry began to sing in a fine clear voice, "I, a tender young maid, have been courted by many..."

"Stop," protested Lydia, laughing. Maisry ignored her. "Of all sorts and trades..."

"Stop!" Lydia collapsed, whooping. She lurched against a wall, gasping for breath. Of course, Maisry continued with the song, and when she started the chorus, Lydia sat down against the wall, bent double. Several fairgoers—mostly young men—had stopped to listen, and were visibly disappointed when Maisry stopped.

"Are you all right?" asked Maisry, not sounding at all concerned. Tears squeezed out from the corners of Lydia's eyes as she swallowed, inhaled deeply, and nodded. She scrubbed her face with a sleeve and exhaled sharply. She raised an eyebrow at Maisry when the maid acted as though she were about to go on to the next verse. Her mouth twitched but she had gotten the laughter under control. Maisry offered a hand, and pulled the other girl up, where she stood, reeling.

Maisry's mouth pursed. "What's wrong?" she asked, more seriously this time. Lydia considered for a moment. "I think I'm drunk," she replied wonderingly. "Good for you!" a man dressed as a cat shouted as he staggered by.

Maisry took a look at the seriously depleted wineskin, then at the still clear eyes of the minstrel. "Why," she said carefully, "should wine make you drunk? What have you been drinking at the palace?"

Lydia shrugged. "Water."

"Water?"

Lydia waved her paper vaguely. "It's good water."

"It should be," muttered the maid. "It's well water, after all. But you shouldn't drink the city water anyway; they get theirs from the river." She wrinkled her nose at the thought.

"And that," Lydia said distinctly, "is why I'm drunk." She smiled, and then looked distressed. "Do people actually do this for fun? I can't imagine why."

"Do you feel sick?" Maisry asked. That would be a rotten end to a festival, though not uncommon. Lydia shook her head, then frowned. "No, not... sick. Just wrong. It's just... wrong." She looked helplessly at the maid, unable to come up with a better description.

She frowned again, studying the bricks of the road. "And that's wrong too." She lifted her head, focusing on a figure on the other side of the foot traffic. "Not a good idea at all." She pushed away from the wall, striding through the crowd, and Maisry trotted along behind.

*   *   *

William was congratulating himself on his strategy. He'd managed to sneak himself and his costume out from the palace, under the very noses of his guards and Captain Dar. He was dressed as a raggedy fool, with ribbons and bells and a patchwork mask, and he was having a marvelous time. The sense of having outwitted his own security was exhilarating.

So it was a complete shock to find his way barred by the blue-clad arm of somebody he recognized. "Greetings, fool," said the minstrel amiably. "You seem to have mislaid your company." A vaguely familiar girl dressed in a nobleman's outfit trotted up, looking confused.

The minstrel couldn't have recognized him. "Noble sir, what can I do for you?" he asked in an ingratiating tone.

Alan's mouth twitched, but he spoke seriously. "This is more than folly," he paused, glancing over at the girl, "*William*." Maisry's eyes widened, but she subsided when the minstrel put out a hand, palm down.

William sighed, rebellious. The minstrel had obviously been having fun. But it was near to impossible to have fun with guards hanging around his neck. He said as much, but the minstrel was shaking his head gently. "Another time, perhaps, but not now. Did you know that the Erleina peasants eat a lot of potatoes?" he said brightly.

William looked at the girl, but she seemed as bewildered as he was. "No," he said, cautiously.

The minstrel was nodding. "D'you know why, then?" He was acting very strangely. William shook his head.

"Potatoes grow underground, so they don't get destroyed when the local battle rides over them. So why do you think there's lots of battles?" he continued cheerfully. William gritted his teeth and said nothing. Alan stopped smiling. "There's been fighting between two collateral branches of the royal line for over sixty years, ever since the last Brightwater king died without heirs." He tilted his head, eyes ever so slightly out of focus. "I have no taste for potatoes."

"You're drunk," William accused.

Alan nodded, and said, "Quite right." He turned toward the girl and tripped over his own feet. William put out a hand that the minstrel shook off, but as the girl looked on with alarm, he started swaying. William ducked and put an arm under the minstrel's shoulders, no mean feat as Alan was a good half-foot shorter than he was. On the other hand, he hardly weighed anything and was easy to support.

He did not notice the wink that the minstrel threw at the girl.

"To the castle, then," the king muttered. He'd known it was hopeless the moment the all-too-perceptive minstrel started to speak, but he'd hoped to get a little dancing in before he had to leave. And Alan had been having a day with a pretty girl—that girl was following along behind, mouth set in a worried line—while William had been cooped up in the castle, thinking on the Erleina ambassador, who was leaving later in the week. There hadn't been any treaties concluded, but the ambassador seemed pleased nonetheless.

The minstrel had started humming as they stumbled along, a tune he didn't recognize. When he glanced over at the girl, she'd blushed bright red across the cheekbones. She ducked her head when she noticed the king looking at her. *Interesting*, William thought.

A sudden thought occurred to him, and he stopped so abruptly that the fairgoers behind him tripped on his heels. "Are you from Erlein?" he asked, curious. The minstrel's reaction wasn't quite what he expected; he slid bonelessly down and dropped to the street, laughing.

"Erlein? You think I'm from Erlein?"

"It was just a thought," William said. *Obviously not a correct one.* Alan shook his head, still laughing, but he took William's proffered hand and rose to his feet.

"Op-por-tu-nis-tic, they are," he said thickly. "Never miss a trick." William had to agree with that assessment.

When they got up to the castle, the girl jumped forward and whispered to the guard, whose eyebrows rose, but who did not bar their way. William wondered what she had said, and if it had even resembled the truth. With any luck, he'd be able to get up to his rooms without too much fuss.

As they passed into the courtyard, the minstrel stumbled, his arm moving up. He straightened in one motion, pulling the king's mask away with a grand gesture. "For your edification, then," he called out gleefully to the guards and other folk in the all-too-busy courtyard. "A drunk and a fool!"

William could feel his face heating. Alan was bowing with no hint of dizziness to the smiling guards. "You..." William began, and stopped when the minstrel put a finger to his lips.

"Ssh. There's one more thing..." He looked up at the battlements. "Ah." He beckoned to the girl. "Maisry." He jerked his head in William's direction. "Kiss him."

The girl shot one shocked look at the minstrel, then smiled, and advanced on the king, doing as she was told to the loud guffaws of the guards. Over her shoulder, William saw the minstrel's careful regard for a moment, and then Alan turned and walked away.

*   *   *

William left his raggedy costume on for dinner. If he couldn't go down to the town for festival, he'd at least try to have a little fun at the palace. Duke Jord frowned; as ever, he was in proper Guardron colors. The silver, black, and deep blue suited his grizzled coloring admirably. But he said nothing as several of the younger courtiers came through in their own gaudy outfits.

Ambassador Liend was a credit to his training; his eyebrows barely twitched as he took in the sight of the king sitting crosswise in his chair. Orrin had informed the king that Erlein did not hold the Festival of Folly, coming as it did in the thick of the growing season. William thought sourly that the ambassador probably hadn't even taken the time to go down and see all the fuss.

When the minstrel entered, William heard a rude comment from further down the table. Alan had also not changed; there was an imprint suspiciously like his sleeve across his face. He bowed to the company and to the king, but instead of retreating to his alcove as he normally did, he walked up to the table. "Ambassador Liend," he said quietly, as every diner turned their eyes to him, "I am afraid that my fingers are tangled. I know you are unfamiliar with our customs, but in honor of the holy day, would you be so kind as to play for us?" He extended his harp.

The ambassador looked uncertain for the first time in William's memory. "I am nowhere near your caliber, Minstrel." Alan kept holding the harp out, his smile gentle.

"This one day we allow folly, Ambassador. Please. I would like to hear you play." When the ambassador finally accepted the harp, Alan walked over and leaned back against the wall.

Liend's fingers brushed the strings uncertainly. He cleared his throat, and asked, "Any requests?" In the silence that followed, the minstrel's quiet reply, "The Loathly Wyrm," was clear and distinct. Liend started to play.

His fingering was uncertain, and the tempo was slow, but he had a basic competence, and after a short intro, the ambassador began to sing.

"When I was seven years old, oh my mother she did die.

My father married the worst woman the world has ever seen;

For she has made me the Loathly Wyrm that lies at the foot of the tree,

And my sister Maisry she's made the Mackerel of the Sea."

William's eyes shot up. The ambassador had a clear tenor voice, and he was obviously used to singing. Even Jord, who hadn't warmed to the man, looked on with approval. As the song of enchantment continued, William wondered what Alan meant by this display. He snuck a look at the minstrel, who in turn was watching the ambassador.

The minstrel refused to play this song that he had requested. The lyrics were not particularly illuminating. The father, upon finding out that his children were enchanted, confronted the lovely wife who had worked the magic. At first, she dissembled, but when he confronted her with her lies, she reversed the spell on the boy. The girl, however, was too wary of the lady, and stayed away.

Liend finished the song with its rather stark ending. The lady was burned for the evils she had done, but the girl remained enchanted. William wondered what message the minstrel was trying to send, and to whom. He blushed when he remembered that the girl in the courtyard had also been named Maisry—you'd think he'd have a better memory for a girl he'd kissed. He was fairly certain the message was not directed at him, though.

When Liend finished, the minstrel levered himself off the wall and walked back. "Thank you, Ambassador," he said mildly. Liend handed over the harp, saying, "It is a lovely instrument."

Alan nodded. "I paid for it myself," he replied. Then he walked over to the alcove and began to play as though nothing had changed.

The diners resumed their meal, satisfied that the show was over. William barely noticed, turning things over in his mind. He wasn't sure if the minstrel were being flippant with his notion of payment or not. It was certainly an odd choice of words.

*   *   *

Lydia awoke in dim light, her window barely distinguishable from the wall. For a moment, she was startled. Then she recalled what woke her. She closed her eyes and concentrated fiercely on the melody that had threaded through her dreams, humming softly until she had the pattern in her mind. She sat up and climbed out of bed, not bothering to light a candle or change out of her nightshirt. She sat on the chest and pulled the harp to her.

She worked out the fingering carefully. *Dreamsong. I've caught a dreamsong!* She played it over and over, hoping to impress the tune into her fingers. Everyone knew how dreams evaporated in the morning light; Lydia knew that if you wanted to catch a bit of dream, you had to get it down right away. This was not the first time she'd heard music in her dreams; in fact, music was a regular feature. But it was rare to have it come out in melody like this and she'd lost songs before.

The room was beginning to lighten as she finally felt the tune making sense to her fingers. She put the harp down and pulled on her livery. The morning bell cut across her hums, dissonant, changing the music, she thought wretchedly. She hoped it was for the better.

Then Lydia remembered the previous day, and gleefully pulled out the paper she had bought. She could write it down and catch it properly.

The music was thrumming across her thoughts now, overlaying everything. It seemed as though she could not forget it, though experience told her otherwise. She stared numbly at the sheets on her table, trying to figure out what was wrong with the picture through a head that was still muzzy with sleep and music.

Paper, paper, paper, she thought. *Paper.*

Pen.

She could have smacked herself, it was so obvious. She had nothing to write with. There were no quills and no ink. She could easily requisition some, she knew, but only much later in the morning. She needed them *now*. But now that she thought on it, she knew where she could get some. Without further thought, she grabbed her paper and strode through the door.

Lydia all but ran into Ambassador Liend as she turned a corner. She looked in dismay at the early riser, running her melody across her thoughts.

"Ah, Minstrel," he said, sinking her spirits. She had to get the music down *now*. "I should like to talk with you."

Go away, go away, she thought madly. She looked up at him, eyes wide and unseeing, and said, "Please, I've got to go." The ambassador frowned, and she said the first thing that sprung to her mind. "I have to catch the dreamsong."

Liend's expression cleared a bit, though Lydia suspected he didn't know what she was babbling about. He stepped aside, and she charged down the corridors. She nodded at the guard and entered the king's study. William wouldn't be in until later in the morning.

But studies have pens. And ink.

*   *   *

"He's already in there, your majesty." said the guard, surprising William. "He has been for hours."

"Minstrel Alan?" William asked. The minstrel usually stopped by in the mid-morning, after he had studied with Master Orrin. When the guard nodded, he creased his forehead. He hoped that Alan wasn't about to start on some new cryptic paranoia. The worries about his safety were bad enough.

He was relieved to enter the room and see the minstrel with his back to the door, writing something. As he walked up, the minstrel stopped, but did not turn to face him. "You're here early," the king said.

"I hope you don't mind," came the reply. William shook his head, then grinned as he realized that Alan couldn't see it. He could just see the tip of the feather as the minstrel tapped it against his cheek.

"I don't mind," he said. "I wasn't very happy with you yesterday, though."

Alan drooped a bit. "It only takes one person—one—lucky enough to get close with a knife, William." He gestured backwards with the pen, and the tip of the feather came to rest on the king's throat.

William swallowed. "I think you just made your point," he said faintly. Alan turned his head, frowning.

The reaction shocked William. Alan turned dead white. He lurched to his feet, and dropped the pen. "For-forgive me, your majesty!" He staggered back and sat, heavily, on an upholstered footstool. Then he covered his face with his hands.

The king bit his lip. Alan had been immoderately cheerful of late, but it didn't always seem right. Sometimes William thought that the minstrel might be putting on a show for him, pretending to be happy so that—*what was the phrase he had used?*—so that seeming could become truth. Sometimes it worked.

William looked at the huddled form on the footstool, and forgave the minstrel for his actions the day before.

He spoke gently. "I don't see what there is to forgive. A feather is not a knife, after all." The minstrel shuddered. "You need not fear that, I think."

Alan took his hands away from his face, but sat slumped, looking at the floor. "I have dreams about it, you know," he said in a flat tone. "A knife in your throat, and me to blame. And blood..." He closed his eyes, shaking his head. "So much blood."

William knew those sorts of dreams. This seemed to be affecting the minstrel a bit more strongly than it should. "It is not something that is going to happen. They are only dreams..."

"I *know* that," Alan replied, a sharp tone to his voice. "That doesn't make them any easier to bear." The minstrel glanced over at the desk, and the papers scattered across the surface. He closed his eyes and exhaled. William straightened up. "Perhaps you should ask Melinda to give you something to help you rest."

Alan rubbed a hand across his face. "...No," he said, faintly. "It's not necessary." He rubbed his fingers along his temples, a gesture that William only saw when the minstrel was stressed. He could have predicted the minstrel's next words. "Who am I, your majesty, that you should take such care of me?"

"If you had forgotten," William replied dryly, "my name is William. And you are the King's Minstrel." He paused, then added, "And my friend." Alan looked up, startled. "A friend who is so concerned for me that he is fretting himself to pieces and why he should do that is beyond me. Especially as he seems to disregard himself when he does so. Have you eaten?" The minstrel, rather shamefaced, shook his head. William waved a hand at the door. "Go. Eat something, for pity's sake. Spend a little of your care on yourself."

When the minstrel had left, he went over to his desk to see what Alan had written. The sheets were covered with the lines and dots that William knew denoted music, though he didn't know how to decipher them. He hoped that someday soon, he would get to hear what they portrayed.

*   *   *

Lydia was still a bit bewildered when the door closed behind her. The pen—ah, Lady be merciful, it had come to rest in the same spot that she'd knifed the brigand. But the strength of her reaction had surprised even her. She thought she had her emotions under control.

Obviously not.

Lydia didn't want to think about the king. He considered her—no, considered *Alan*—a friend. He trusted her far too much for his own safety, and she couldn't make him see that, not without revealing who she actually was. That was unthinkable for a varying number of reasons. She had to play this masquerade into the ground. She gritted her teeth and turned her steps towards the kitchen. Maybe food would help her think this through.

With a shock, she realized that the pasties of the day before had been the last thing she'd eaten. She'd slept through her own dinner—not even lying down, and she'd almost been late—she'd been too keyed up to think of food afterwards. *No wonder I'm out of sorts.*

When Ambassador Liend turned up in her path, she looked at him in irritation. Of *course* he'd be standing in between her and food. He'd already gotten in her way once this morning. "Did you catch the... ah... dreamsong, then?" he asked, gently.

Lydia blinked. The music—the humming, insistent music—had disappeared from her thoughts, as she'd predicted. She couldn't, for the moment, even recall what it had been. An instant of worry was replaced by a mental image of page after page filled with notations—*left in the king's study*, she thought wryly. Though how she'd managed to get it down was a bit of a blur to her. She'd never had such a prolonged fit of inspiration before.

"I think so, Ambassador," she said carefully. She was not in a position to needle this man, much as she'd like to crack his well-cultivated facade.

"I should like to speak with you," the ambassador said, just as he had this morning. Lydia would have liked to put him off, at least until she could have something to eat, but she'd already done so once. With a mental sigh, she said, "Of course, Ambassador."

The ambassador led the way to the formal gardens on the north side of the castle. The full sun startled Lydia somewhat; she'd been in the study for hours. And she'd never been in the gardens before. She wasn't barred from them, but there hadn't been any need to frequent them. *Admit it*, she told herself sternly, *it was too much like leaving the castle.*

She eyed the ambassador carefully. He might be anywhere from thirty to fifty with that face, though the amber hair, unstreaked by gray, argued towards the lower number. As always, he was dressed in a formal court robe, this one in shades of brown and cream and hints of dull red that flattered his coloring. Not for the first time, Lydia wondered if his looks were a help or a hindrance.

Of course, when there were so few ladies at the court, his looks might not matter either way. As for Lydia herself, well, she was so unable to trust the man that his looks didn't seem to affect her at all. Except— now that she thought on it—she'd been wary of him the first time she saw him. That made her wonder.

When he led her into a grotto, screened by hedges, Lydia began to worry. Just a bit, though. You never knew when a gardener might be nearby and surely the capable Liend would not provoke an incident.

"The offer still stands," he stated without preamble. "I should very much like to hire you on, Minstrel Alan."

Lydia let out a breath she didn't know she'd been holding. "I am sorry, Ambassador." In a way, she was sorry; Liend's fascination for music was the one unfeigned reaction she'd ever seen from the man. "I belong here."

The ambassador paced. "Here, where they treat you like a servant? Here, where they don't give you the respect you deserve?"

Here, where I am home. The thought startled Lydia. "I made a promise, and I will not go back on it. I cannot be other than I am," she added.

Liend stopped pacing, and looked at her squarely. "What are you, then?"

"King's Minstrel," she said faintly. A girl in boy's clothing, if Liend had the wit to see it. What if he did, and tried to use that information? She would have nowhere to hide.

"King's Minstrel," Liend repeated, and looked disgusted. "That's it, isn't it. You belong to him and he doesn't even know what you are."

"What I am?" Lydia repeated in turn. *What did he see?*

"Don't you know how rare a talent you have, Minstrel?" Lydia relaxed, fractionally. "I know the songs, and I know what you have played. Will you deny that over half of your songs are your own?" Lydia shook her head, perplexed. Why would she deny something so obvious? The ambassador took her by her shoulders. "You have a gift, Minstrel Alan, a gift for some of the sweetest melodies I have ever heard. And this morning—it was as though you had been touched by the Singer himself. Can you not see why I am loath to leave you here, where they think of you as... as a mere performer?"

Sweet Lady bright, he was acting as though she were a saint. She drew a ragged breath. "Are all Erleina as fervent as you?" Surely not.

Liend frowned. He released her shoulders as he straightened. "No. Not so..." He cut himself off. "I have at least one sister who never had an ear for music. But that is neither here nor there." He looked at her with level eyes. "You won't accept, will you."

"No, Ambassador," she replied, smiling faintly. He sighed somewhat theatrically. "Perhaps I shall hear you play, then, when I am sent here again."

"Perhaps you shall, Ambassador," Lydia replied.

Lydia watched him leave and sat down on a bench, kicking her heels. She wondered, again, if the ambassador were all that he seemed. It seemed somehow excessive, his interest in one solitary minstrel. She sucked in her breath as she remembered the king's voice that morning, calling her a friend. Had Liend somehow seen that, and thought to use it as leverage? But for what?

She waited for a time, wanting the ambassador to get well ahead before returning to the castle. So at first her sun-dazzled eyes were unwilling to admit that there was someone in the doorway, waiting for her. It was not the ambassador, but a smaller shadow—one whose height was creeping towards her own with astonishing swiftness.

"Jankin?" Lydia asked. "What are you about?"

The page looked a bit rueful. "I was waiting for you, Minstrel. Master Orrin set me to find you."

"Orrin? Why would he..." Lydia trailed off. The sun was quite high now, shading toward noontime. She blanched. "Oh. Oh dear." She'd completely missed her lesson.

Jankin shifted uncertainly. "You'll come, won't you? Master Orrin is very sarcastic when he's vexed."

Lydia nodded. "I'll go. You can go back to whatever you were doing before Master Orrin showed his… ah… vexation." The page bounced off with no further encouragement. Lydia's own paces were somewhat slower, but not quite funereal.

It was rather a shock, then, to find Orrin's mood as outwardly calm as ever. "Ah. Minstrel. There you are."

"Master Orrin, I am so sorry..." He cut off her apology with a graceful wave. "Conor told me that the Erleina ambassador wished to have speech with you. You spoke with the ambassador?" She nodded. "Then I shall overlook the missed lesson."

Lydia flushed. "I was not speaking with the ambassador when I missed the lesson, Master Orrin. I was in the king's study." *Better to have that out in the open*, she thought.

Orrin's expression did not alter. "Did you never wonder why we spend so much time on your education, and on the education of the pages?" Lydia nodded. "It is to make use of the minds and talents of those who may serve in less obvious ways than the nobility. How the king chooses to use those talents is his concern." He looked at her sharply. "You missed your lesson because the ambassador wished to speak with you."

Lydia blinked. This was the first indication she had had that her meetings with the king were a minor secret. "So," she said slowly, "It is not to be generally known that the king... wishes music in the mornings?"

The Master of Protocol gave a tight smile. "Exactly so," he said quietly. Then he sighed. "In truth, you are so mind-hungry that I was worried that something ill had befallen you."

Lydia held very still. *Mind-hungry?* The word 'hungry' conjured up uncomfortable images, and a reminder from her stomach, but she didn't understand his meaning. "Everyone is so protective of me." She shot a sharp glance towards the seated man. "Why?"

Master Orrin leaned forward, searching her face. "When you played last night, how many nobles were at the dinner?"

She counted in her mind. "There were three tables, and there were... Oh!" She thought back to her first weeks at the castle. "The hall was almost full. But what has that to do with me?"

Orrin leaned back, shaking his head with a slight smile. "Anything else that you noticed?"

"There were not many ladies," she replied, frowning slightly. "Mostly older nobles, such as our Lord Duke of Guardron. He has three sons, does he not?" At Orrin's nod, she continued: "So they run the Duchy quite well in his absence. And they send the older men to court, to work in their favor, and the younger sons. But they do not attend themselves. There are no entertainments, no call for them to come in..." She trailed off as she took in the expression on Master Orrin's face. "What?"

"I ask you one question, and you reply, and think of the effects of that reply, and move on to figuring a solution without pausing for breath. Mind-hungry, as I said. Do you think that no one notices what you do?" Orrin asked.

"Do?" replied Lydia faintly. "I don't do much of anything but play the harp."

Orrin looked at her, narrowing his eyes. "You value yourself too lightly, Minstrel Alan." A touch of acid tinged his next words. "We learn as we are taught, I suppose." He took in the confused expression on her face. "A lecture for another time. I wanted to speak with you for a different reason." He nodded towards the familiar, simple chair. Lydia sank into it gratefully and looked up expectantly. "You spoke, a moment ago, of entertainments. Part of your duty is to obtain such."

"Obtain... You mean hire?"

Orrin gave a slight frown. "Melinda will do the actual hire. I mean more in the sense of giving trial, to determine who is good enough." Lydia swallowed. Master Orrin smiled and shook his head. "Normally, it is merely a matter of hearing the musicians play; they present themselves at the gate. There is a group here now."

Lydia looked up, startled. "Here? Now?" It shouldn't have surprised her, she knew. She had wondered herself at the lack of musicians. She rubbed suddenly nerveless palms down her legs. "Master Orrin, what do I do?" she asked plaintively.

Orrin folded his hands. "Why, Minstrel, you do what you know best. Go and listen to their music." She stood, bowed, and half-ran from the room. Orrin looked after her, and dipped his pen to write another cryptic note.

*   *   *

Lydia made her way down to the courtyard, looking around the usual midday bustle of deliveries. When she did not see any musicians, she asked the guard at the gate, who told her that they had been taken directly to the server's hall. She hurried towards it, then stopped and straightened her clothing. She had an image to present.

She stopped dead outside the hall itself. She could hear, through the open door, the strains of a song she had never heard before. She heard gittern, flute, tambour, and a female singer. The song itself held unfamiliar cadences, reminiscent of the island kingdom of Leneara. Unwilling to interrupt, she moved on silent feet to the door.

They were good. With a small pang, Lydia realized that she had never learned to play in concert with others. These obviously had, as musical embroideries swung from one instrument to another. Just before the last chorus, the gittern and flute stopped playing; this drew out the tension for four beats until they began again. It brought an extra emphasis to the final lines. Stomps and whistles greeted the end of the song, and Lydia moved into the doorway.

There were three of them, standing at the far end. The gittern player had brown curly hair over a squarish face that was likewise brown. The flautist was tall and thin and had longish dark hair. His flute was of black wood with metal keys. It must have cost a small fortune.

It was the singer who drew Lydia's eyes, however. She was likewise tall, and had straight black hair that fell, unbound, in a curtain down her back. The tambour was held in hands that were graceful and delicate, and some of the appreciative stares in the room were for her beauty, not her singing.

Lydia felt a twinge of jealousy, which she ruthlessly suppressed.

It was the gittern player who noticed her, standing in the doorway. He nudged the flautist and pointed. The various servants who had disposed themselves around the room looked back, saw the minstrel, and started to leave. The flautist walked over to Lydia.

"Are you to take us to the Minstrel?" he asked, with a hint of boredom in his voice. "We should like to perform before too much longer."

Lydia looked past him at the other two. The gittern player was looking rather thoughtful, while the girl seemed amused at the flautist's haughty behavior. "What did you call what you were just doing, then?" she asked. He must have taken her for a page.

"Mere rehearsal," the flautist replied loftily, and the girl said cheerfully,

"Give it up, Tem, the lad's not impressed with your manner."

Tem relaxed. Conspiratorially, he asked, "It was good, wasn't it?"

Lydia laughed. "Yes, it was good. It was good enough to impress the Minstrel." She gave him an impish smile. "Not the haughty manner, though. That doesn't go over well."

Tem looked sheepish. "Sometimes, it's the only thing that does. Lead on, then!"

"Here is good enough," Lydia replied. She hopped up and sat on one of the tables and waved Tem back towards the group. The gittern player smothered a laugh at Tem's expression, while the girl said, "Tem, you dolt, that IS the Minstrel."

"Eri..." Tem looked back at the girl.

Eri shot him a withering glance. "My brainless cousin over there is a good musician but has all the tact of a goat."

"I'm not your cousin, I'm your brother," he protested.

"It's times like these I want to disclaim the relationship," she countered. She eyed Lydia thoughtfully. "I thought you'd be older."

"I thought he'd be taller," added Tem.

"You think everyone should be as tall as you," Eri replied.

"And you do not, little sister?" he countered.

"Do they always go on like this?" Lydia asked the gittern player. The siblings both closed their mouths pointedly.

The gitternist smiled and replied, "Constantly. My name's Jessen, by the way. No relation to these two nitwits."

"Nitwits!?" they protested in chorus.

Lydia swung her feet, hands on the edge of the table. it was all she could do to keep from grinning. "Since we've established that, perhaps you could play me a song?" she asked. She was inclined to hire them, but there was no need to let them know that.

Eri looked back at the other two. Jessen struck a chord, experimentally, and Eri nodded. They launched into a more flowing piece than the one Lydia had heard from the hallway. After a short intro, Eri began to sing.

"There are suitors at my door,
Oh le-lay-o bah-i-a,
Six or eight or even more,
Oh le-lay-o bah-i-a.
And my father wants me wed,
Oh le-lay-o bah-i-a,
Or at least that's what he said.
Oh le-lay-o bah-i-a."

Lydia let her grin escape. This song was definitely from the island, by the sound of it. Leneara girls were notoriously choosy. Eri sang the nonsense words of the chorus in a flowing manner, echoed by the flute. It was strangely compelling. Lydia wondered, idly, if there were a dance that went with the song, then decided, upon second thought, that if there were, she didn't want to know about it.

> *"And I told him that I will*
> *Oh le-lay-o bah-i-a,*
> *When the rivers run uphill,*
> *Oh le-lay-o bah-i-a.*
> *And the fish begin to fly,*
> *Oh le-lay-o bah-i-a,*
> *And the day before I die,*
> *Oh le-lay-o bah-i-a."*

Lydia's fingers itched. She could hear exactly where a harp would fit into what they were playing.

> *"Streams a-backwards run uphill,*
> *Oh le-lay-o bah-i-a,*
> *Fish are flying with a will.*
> *Oh le-lay-o bah-i-a.*
> *And today's the day I wed,*
> *Oh le-lay-o bah-i-a,*
> *And tomorrow I'll be dead.*
> *Oh le-lay-o bah-i-a."*

Lydia's smile disappeared abruptly. As the chorus wound to a close, she bit her lip and wondered quite how to phrase it. Eri took note of her expression, and the moment the music stopped, she asked, worriedly, "You don't like it?"

"It's beautiful," Lydia replied truthfully. "But... it's a rather grim ending, isn't it?"

Eri and Tem exchanged glances. Jessen smacked his forehead. "Now I'm the nitwit," he stated. "Don't you two remember the last time we came through?" A dawning look of comprehension appeared on the girl's face. Tem still looked confused. "We didn't get a trial," he complained.

"We didn't get a trial because the lady the prince loved had died," Jessen replied. "She played the harp." He blinked and looked at Lydia. She spread her hands.

"As do I, as I guess you have heard," she said. She looked at the hesitant look on the girl's face and decided to not draw it out any longer. "What term were you seeking?"

"Two weeks, and then we head west," replied the gittern player. He looked to be somewhat older than the other two.

Lydia tilted her head slightly. "Might you be back through the city at the end of summer?" she asked. The song, subtly disturbing though it was, had given her an idea.

Jessen was smiling. "We might, if there were any work to be had."

Lydia jumped off the table. "You are certainly a talented crew. Do you have any more new songs?"

Eri shook her head. "Just that and The Wild Dance, which you heard before. Are there any other songs to avoid?"

Lydia flushed. "Rosemary, Thistle, and Thorn." She didn't bother to explain. Jessen regarded her thoughtfully.

As she turned, she saw Melinda standing in the back of the hall. She smiled in relief that she wouldn't have to track her down. "Melinda will discuss the terms of your hire," she said, glad that somebody else would do the bargaining. She had no idea what musicians were to be paid.

Melinda folded her arms. "Melinda will also send you to the kitchen, Minstrel," she said. On cue, Lydia's stomach made a loud sound of protest. She turned an embarrassed smile towards the siblings, who made relieved shooing motions at her.

Lydia took the hint and departed towards her long-delayed meal.

*　　*　　*

Duke Jord seemed pleased to hear the new group playing in the evening. "Finally, we get some singing," he muttered. The king looked at him, fork empty.

"What do you have against Minstrel Alan?" he asked, not quite idly. The Guardron lord seemed to dislike the youth, a feeling that was not reciprocated. Alan referred to the Duke as "one of the most loyal lords you could wish to have."

Jord snorted. "He's too slippery," he replied. "He's hiding something. A man cannot hide his soul when he sings."

William looked over at the minstrel, who was leaning forward, ankle on his knee, and a look of rapt concentration on his face. "Look," he said quietly, and gestured with his fork. Jord turned, saw the intense look, then glanced up at the attractive singer in the gallery. He snorted. "Lovestruck," he said.

"In love with the music," interjected ambassador Liend rather sourly. The other men looked at him in surprise. Liend spread his hands. William turned back to see that Alan had closed his eyes, listening intently to the music.

*   *   *

The minstrel was exiting the hall when a shadow detached itself to stand over him. "Walk with me, minstrel," said Duke Jord. After a startled bow, Alan followed. Jord made a few turns, to give them privacy, then stopped in the middle of a disused room. "What game are you playing, Minstrel?" he asked, turning abruptly.

Alan shrunk back, leaning into the shadows. "My lord Duke," he began, and then stopped, took a breath and began again. "I don't know what you mean," he said, faintly.

Jord narrowed his eyes. "You baffle me. You're a minstrel, but you don't sing—and I've heard some very bad singers, so don't give me that excuse. Everyone at this castle seems to think well of you. Even my own servants speak about you. You have the most widespread allies. It's as though you have the castle beglamoured." Alan swallowed. "But nobody knows a thing about you before you came here. What are you hiding?"

"My lord, it is of little consequence," the minstrel began.

"You're lying."

"Then it is of great consequence, and I had rather not say it," replied the minstrel lightly, though there was a faint line between his brows. Jord stepped closer to him, and he closed his eyes, almost wincing. Jord studied his face carefully. There was a hint of familiarity in those features.

"You remind me of Kentwell," he mused aloud. The minstrel's eyes snapped open even as his face flushed.

"I would rather," Minstrel Alan said between clenched teeth, "tear my heart out *myself* than become another such as he. Good *day*, my Lord Guardron." He stormed past Jord, but stopped, shoulders slumped, when Jord called him back.

"I meant," Jord said, more quietly, "that you have a hint of the Kentwell features about you, not that you reminded me of the traitor. Is it that you are a by-blow? That should not shame you to the point of utter secrecy."

Without turning around, the minstrel said, "I knew both father and mother. They are dead now. Though I desire your good opinion, Duke Jordeth, I cannot do other than as I have done."

"And what have you done?" *Other than dodge all of my questions quite neatly*, the Duke mused.

The minstrel turned. "All I have done is for the king," he said with utter sincerity. "If you believe nothing else, please believe that." He swept a bow. "My lord Duke." He walked away, back as straight as an arrow, each step placed as precisely as a dance. Jord was not sure if the stiffness was due to anger or to fear.

*　　*　　*

The chapel windows shone strangely in the dark of night. Sean paused in his trek toward his bunk and looked carefully at the leaded glass. The light flickered a bit, as of a candle in the darkened interior. Curious now, the guard entered the hallway to look in the open door.

A slight figure, hatless, was a silhouette in front of a single candle. Sean could hear the light murmured prayer, distinct for all its quietness.

"...motólol baranjánka tol. Á lash darán. Lash darán."

Lash darán. *Give me strength*. It was a variant of the traditional prayer before battle, but the guard only knew the standard prayers, and could not decipher the rest of the plea. He stepped quietly into the chapel, walking up to the figure tucked away in an unfinished niche. The stark rock pillars formed an eerie grotto for prayer, a somewhat disconcerting choice. But there was the minstrel, sitting on feet in a manner that looked extremely uncomfortable to Sean. Alan was slightly hunched, arms wrapped around his middle instead of crossed over chest, as would be proper for prayer.

Sean looked carefully at Alan, who seemed aware of his presence, but who did not move. He no longer thought of the minstrel as a feral animal. Instead, he was reminded of a horse his father had bought once, which had the scars of a previous owner on its hide. Through patient training, his father had turned it from a horse that shied at any sudden movement to a gelding that could be counted on to give a smooth ride to any lady—but he never had managed to train it to accept any male but him in the saddle.

There was, about the minstrel, a stillness that spoke of that same well-restrained panic. The other guards might speak of how relaxed Alan had become. Sean could see, sometimes, how much of an effort it cost the minstrel to appear so.

After a long moment, Alan looked up and said, "I guess it isn't worthwhile to wait for you to speak first." Sean had to smile as he sat down. Alan had a gift with words, a talent for phrasing, something Sean always despaired of acquiring for himself. Words turned to mud in his mouth and he found that saying little was preferable to saying the wrong thing. The guard could, with effort, speak as he wished to speak, but normal conversation moved too fast for him to keep up.

But as Alan looked up with no hint of impatience, Sean found that he could think of the right thing to say after all. "If you wish to talk, I will listen."

"...and not say a word about it? Thank you," the minstrel replied thoughtfully. "It is a wonderful gift you offer." A pause, and then the minstrel sighed. "Sometimes, I think I shall strangle on secrecy, and yet..." Alan looked up, pupils matching in the dim light. "If I could tell anyone, I could tell you. But I think it is too big to be told. And yet it's such a little thing..."

"Who you are." It was not a question. On impulse, Sean added, "Girl."

Her smile was sudden and bright, a flash of teeth that showed a more carefree past. "Who I *was*, actually." She unfolded her legs from beneath her and drew her knees up to her chest. "Even if I could freely speak my name, I think the girl I was died long ago."

Sean had a memory of gray skies and knife-edged cold. "In Ellidar?" he asked gently.

"In Ellidar, in Ellidar, bright jewel of Rooke..." Alan half-sang. "No. It was long before that." She subsided into a silence that was almost companionable, watching the wax of the candle being drawn up into the wick. Just when Sean thought the minstrel was done, she stirred and said, "Far to the north, beyond the borders, there's a desert. Nobody's ever bothered to claim it, though trading companies pass through there." She bit her lip, thinking.

"I once spoke to a man who told me of the streams that flow in the desert, little muddy rills at the bottoms of huge crevasses," she continued. "Sometimes there wouldn't be any water at all, just a cracked floor of dried mud. Yet there would be walls five times the height of a man, and twice as wide." Alan stared at the candle. Sean stared at the minstrel. As far as he knew, this was the first time the minstrel had so much as hinted at a past. She went on: "He said that there are times—sunny days, not a cloud in the sky, and hot—when the riverbed will flow with a sudden wave of water. The Lord alone knows where it comes from. He saw a man die that way once, caught in the bottoms with his mule."

The minstrel paused again, and for once, Sean saw someone else's struggle with finding the right words. "If—if you didn't know what they were, you could be deceived by the little streams. They're dangerous, sudden, and strong." She sighed. "Sometimes I feel as though I am standing on those banks, warning of the impending wave, yet everyone else sees only the mud. It's enough to make one doubt one's memories." She rubbed her fingers together, thoughtfully, as though seeking a tangible reminder of the truth of her words. "I'm running out of time, you see. It won't be too much longer before it's obvious that I'm not a boy. And I know the water's coming."

Sean shivered. Prophets are so seldom believed. The minstrel—whose unspoken past might hint at the dangerous and deadly games of the nobility—was implying that the secrecy of her rank played into a larger game, one that might well involve all that knew her. He also knew something else, something she had not told him, that was undoubtedly central to her fears.

He'd seen them in the courtyard. She'd made sure he'd seen. And though he couldn't be happy at the thought of Maisry kissing anyone else, what caught at his heart was the expression on the minstrel's face as she had sent another girl to do what she could not.

"What will you do then?" he asked, finally. Alan looked up with a smile that did not reach her eyes.

"I will do what Martin has told me to do all along, when he teaches me to defend myself." She stretched her arms out before her, then rose to her feet.

"I am going to move in an unexpected direction."

Goldeneyes the Scullion

I have a song to sing, O!
    Sing me your song, O!
It is sung with a sigh
and a tear in the eye
For it tells of a righted wrong, O!
It's a song of a merrymaid, once so gay,
Who turned on her heel and tripped away
From the peacock poppinjay, bravely born
Who turned up his noble nose with scorn
At the humble heart that he did not prize:
So she begged on her knees, with downcast eyes,
For the love of the merryman, moping mum,
Whose soul was sad, and whose glance was glum,
Who sipped no sup, and who craved no crumb,
As he sighed for the love of a ladye!

The slow unfolding of that year's summer had the flavor of the miraculous to Lydia. The summers of Kentwell were parched affairs, with the vegetation bleaching out in the sun. All of her childhood memories were of dazzling gold summers, sunlight so bright it hurt the eyes, the scent of ripening grain and dust. There was an orchard belonging to the keep, carefully irrigated, and the summer fruits were best eaten straight off the tree, hot with sun and heavy with scent.

So it was a bit startling to her to realize that summer was well underway, yet the land remained green, a green so intense it hardly seemed real. The weather turned warm, and sometimes even hot, but rarely reached the ovenlike temperatures Lydia remembered. And even in the summer, rain fell—rain, or a mist so fine you could hardly believe it was falling. She tried to remember the previous summer, the feel of the land, but her memories blurred into the overwhelming sense of need, and seemed somehow dingy, colorless in the face of the wonder before her.

The wonder extended even to the kitchen. The hay berry season was later, and stayed longer, and Lydia wangled quite a few of the delectable red fruit. Brambleberries she knew, though the local variety was bigger and sweeter—and thornier, she was told. They had a similar berry that they called caneberries, and one day she entered the kitchen to see a large basket of small blue-gray globes that she was told were "starfruit." She cautiously tried one, and then gleefully scooped up a handful, much to the laughter of the cooks.

"You do know that that's commonly called Ladysberry, don't you?" chuckled Paige, as Lydia kept working her way through the basket happily. "A help to women."

"I don't *care,*" Lydia replied. Marta eventually had to chase her out of the kitchen with a wooden spoon. When the berries started appearing in the king's study every morning, she kept the reason—and the fruit—to herself.

She'd never had to use the expedient of rags that she had worried about. Shortly after the Festival of Folly, a corsetlike garment appeared in her clothes chest. It was an affair that was well-designed to strap chests flat. The lacings were looped and easily tightened without assistance.

It was not, by any means, a new garment.

Eri, Tem and Jessen had left after their agreed term, but were quickly succeeded by a procession of musicians, bards, and traveling songsters. Lydia hardly played a solo night after word had spread, and some nights she didn't play at all. Most of those who presented themselves were of acceptable quality. Those who were not, she had to inform, gently or firmly, that they should seek their coin elsewhere. A few she would take aside, and question for the news they brought. Some were sent off with bread, or fruit. Very rarely she would give coin, and instructions—usually when she saw something in their eyes she didn't like.

*   *   *

Orrin folded his hands and looked at Lydia carefully. "In terms of history," he said carefully, "I do not think there is anything left to teach you."

Lydia looked startled, and protested, "There is so much I do not know..."

Orrin cut her off. "That is not the point. You are already better at finding things out than any student I have ever had, and in the main, your grasp is as complete as any noble would have the right to expect."

Lydia blinked, slowly. In all honesty, she had never bothered to consider her own level of competence, and only thought of how every time she learned something new, it brought up ten more questions to be answered. "I... see," she replied, slowly. "What do you suggest?"

Master Orrin regarded her thoughtfully across the table. "I thought you might speak with me about some of the information you have been extracting from the various musicians you have been interviewing. Primarily those you have been bribing."

Lydia thought grimly that nothing the Protocol Master did should surprise her. She had never seen him outside of this study, but his sources of information were legendary. "Not... bribes, actually," she said. "More in the line of payment for good observation and," she sighed, "requests for more. So far the information isn't anything in particular, but a little work now may lead to timely words later."

Orrin nodded. "Go on."

"Guardron is doing particularly well this year; a shipwright figured out a new coating for their ships which seems to retard rot and barnacles. They've had fewer ships out for repair in the last two summers and the catch is phenomenal. Duke Jordeth has taught his sons thoroughly, and may well go into a permanent court retirement, which is a pity. He's too skilled to be wasted. Kerril has not sent a representative to court because they have had some tricky dealings with pirates in the last few seasons and the best courtiers also happen to be the most successful fighters. That's rare," she commented, in an unusual burst of annoyance at the fluttering court moths.

"Sherr and Beechen are, unsurprisingly, the same as they ever were. There's the usual level of grumbling in half a dozen of the southern duchies and baronies, where they would be upset if anything actually did change. And there's drought in the north," she added.

Orrin raised one elegant eyebrow at her tone of voice. "Is not drought a serious thing?" he asked.

She sighed. "There's always drought in the north, at least as you would understand it. People around here are worried if it doesn't rain for a week, but it can go the whole summer without rain past the mountains. There are aqueducts and ditches. Coopers never want for work. So yes, there's drought, but nothing that hasn't been dealt with before."

"Were there not floods this spring?" he reminded her.

Lydia felt a crawling foreboding across the back of her neck. "There were, weren't there," she said carefully. Orrin leaned back in his chair, and waved one hand. "I should like to hear your thoughts on what will happen," he said. "That will be your new challenge, instead of history."

She compressed her lips together for a moment, arranging her thoughts. "It seems to me," she began, "that the floods in the spring were warm rain just at the thaw. So the floods were not only the heavy rain, but part of the summer water. Fields turn to mud, and others overgrow their capacity. There would be too many plants with shallow roots, and then the sun would dry them out. I don't like this," she said abruptly. "The crops from this year might be half or less of a regular year."

"Famine," Orrin said concisely.

Lydia shook her head. "Shortages, not famine. The roads are good, are they not? And there is always trade." She remembered one winter of fish and strange dried meat, where every meal tasted somewhat foreign. "Accommodations can be made."

"Which accommodations are those?" he prompted.

"That entirely depends on last year's crop, and the management of the duchies in question. If they had good years, and stored against future need, then nothing will need to be done." She fell silent.

"And if not?" Orrin asked, gently.

"If not," she continued slowly, "then, they will have to send representatives to court, to request aid. It is better that they should come sooner, rather than later, if that is the case. Such things take time to arrange."

"You have doubts," the Protocol Master observed. Lydia looked at him sourly. He never missed a thing, and she was certain that he had a fairly good idea of what she was, if not, in particular, *who*.

"I have my doubts," she agreed. "A well-managed duchy will have stores for years, while a poorly-managed one will not. But if a duchy is normally prosperous, a mediocre managing will mask the troubles until it is late—and a mediocre manager may not understand the looming crisis."

Orrin leaned forward again, and looked straight at her eyes. "What would you suggest be done, then?"

She was silent for a long moment. This could be the sort of mental exercise given to a good student, yet she had the dawning suspicion that Orrin was not only going to take her ideas seriously, but that he was going to act on them as though she were the one to set policy.

But then, if it were the sensible thing to do, why should he not take her advice? "If it is likely that aid will be asked for too late, then I should prepare to give it, that it might be sent the moment it is asked for." Orrin nodded. "Aid best comes from a nearby duchy, the nearer the better, and one that has had a good year."

"Guardron."

"Guardron," she agreed. She had little doubt that the Lord Duke would be in charge of a relief party, and the thought gave her some comfort. Out of the palace, he couldn't discover who she was.

And if the relief party were to be necessary, he was a lord who would not be fooled.

*   *   *

"So," said the king one morning, "I hear that I am holding a ball."

The minstrel was seated sideways in an upholstered armchair, one leg swinging freely. He took an arm-length pipe from his lips as he grinned wildly. "You hear correctly. I had wondered how long rumor would take to run so high." He tilted his head back and smiled at the ceiling. William looked at Alan in sour amusement. The minstrel was obviously pleased with himself, and probably all the more so at having outmaneuvered the king.

He certainly had managed to keep his preparations secret for an appallingly long time. When William had been asked about the ball—by a noble visiting from the far south, no less—he'd dissembled, directing the man to Melinda. Then he had gone to that lady himself. She'd informed him that Alan had started planning at the beginning of summer, months gone. How he'd managed to hire on a full roster of entertainment without starting rumors—at least, that William had heard—and to bespeak provisions for the descending horde was a mystery.

The damnable minstrel was still grinning. William said, "So what is the purpose of this exhibition, anyway? To parade me in front of my people, so that they know I can dress like any preening bird? To show them I can spend money with the best of them?"

Alan closed his eyes and said, dreamily, "To find you a wife, of course. You can hardly screen the ladies of the kingdom one at a time. This way, they can fall upon you all at once and tear each other to shreds to get at you."

William muttered, "I hardly need a wife, what with you arranging my life to suit you."

The most extraordinary expression passed over the minstrel's face. Then he blinked, and put the pipe back to his lips. The tune he played was a straightforward rendition of "The Merry Man and His Maid," and William started grinning as he got to the line about the "peacock poppinjay." It was hard to stay annoyed with the minstrel, even when Alan pulled a trick of this magnitude on him.

"I think I know how I shall punish you," he remarked as the song drew to a close. "You will come to the ball and find the right lady for me."

Alan sat upright and swiveled to face the king, a look of astonishment on his face. "What?"

William smiled. The minstrel looked mildly panicked. *A just punishment indeed.* "As I said. We will dress you up as a peacock poppinjay and you shall dance with the ladies and see if any will meet your high standards." The minstrel looked worried. The king thought for a moment. "You do dance, don't you?"

"Uh... yes," the minstrel replied reluctantly. He opened his mouth to object and William broke in with, "Don't try to say you'll be busy. According to Melinda, you've hired enough musicians to play for a week." The king deliberately tilted his head, the way Alan did when he was being witty. "Where did you think you would be, when the music was playing and the ladies were dancing?"

Alan, blank-faced, said, "Out in front, spreading pitch on the stairs."

William stared for a minute, and then broke into laughter. He collapsed onto a footstool, still laughing, and looked up to see the minstrel's mouth twitching. "You're very single-minded sometimes," he told Alan. "You decided I had to be married when we first met and you've been working toward that ever since."

"Well, your majesty," Alan declaimed, rising to his feet, "I cannot defend you with my skill." He took a parody of a fighting stance, wielding his pipe as a makeshift sword. "I cannot rouse armies to your aid." He straightened up to his full height, which was definitely shy of average. He looked down at himself with a light smile. "I can hardly intimidate your opponents on the field or in the chamber, but I can endeavor to make you aware of your best interests. I am, and remain, your most obedient servant and minstrel." He bowed elaborately, pulling off and flipping his hat in an exaggerated courtier's bow. He straightened up, reversing the flip deftly.

"Do you practice that bow in front of a mirror?" William asked.

"Just in my mind," Alan replied. He fell back into the chair and leaned on one arm. "I haven't looked in a mirror for some time."

"What, are you afraid of magic mirrors?"

The minstrel smiled. "All mirrors are magic," he replied wryly. "But no, I just haven't had occasion."

"Perhaps you ought," returned the king. "You might find some admirers of your own at the ball." In truth, he never would have expected the bony lad of spring to look so well. Alan's face would always be lean, but months of good food and warm living had brought his features into harmony. More than one maid might fall for the youth with the golden-brown eyes. Even if those eyes all too often held a skeptical expression, as they did now. "You will come, will you not?" he asked.

"Do I have a choice?"

"Not really," William said.

"Well then," the minstrel said in resignation, "as this is a duty I cannot escape, perhaps it would be best if you were to tell me what, exactly, you are looking for."

The king opened and shut his mouth a few times, and Alan burst out in laughter. "You hadn't thought about it, had you?" The minstrel went on, shaking his head, "I have been nagging you for months, as you say, and you never bothered to think about what you would want in a wife."

"I... I'll know it when I meet her," William said, with a weak smile. Alan stopped laughing, and looked at the king curiously. "Do you really believe in love at first sight?"

William stopped smiling abruptly. "I did," he replied flatly.

"Oh. *Oh*. William, I am sorry." To his credit, Alan really did look contrite, as though he really had, for once, not meant to prod.

The king shook his head. "You need not apologize. You're right that I should not be so sensitive on the subject." He looked up, an appeal in his eyes, and the minstrel took the hint.

"Very well then, we shall find out your perfect wife. Hair and eye color?" he asked brightly, a twinkle in his eyes. William looked at him with a gravity that was already eroding. "Height and weight, perhaps? Would you like a wife you can look in the eyes, or one you can throw over your shoulder?" The minstrel sprang to his feet. "Or we may be going about this all wrong. It should not be a ball; it should be a dragon, and a lady in a tower..."

Still seated, William folded his arms and crooked an eyebrow at the youth. "I think I should do fairly well with a lady I can talk to."

Alan grinned. "That's a start."

"You have told me, time and again, that I need not love the lady I marry, but I should at least like to be friends with her."

"*Very* good. I may become a teacher yet."

William considered sticking his tongue out at the minstrel, but that would only underscore his point. "I'd like to find a lady who has something in the way of wits. I can't stand the idea of a dull queen who only understands the empty games of court."

"That's not so difficult," the minstrel said lightly. "A good many noble daughters find it... expedient … to pretend they are stupider than they are. Go on."

William looked at the minstrel, mildly surprised. "Well, I should like a lady who gets along with the Royal Minstrel," he added.

Alan looked baffled, and a little worried. "Why?"

The king frowned. "Why should I not want someone who appreciates my friends?" He was more than a little tired of the minstrel's self-effacing ways. And sure enough, the minstrel began, "But who am I..."

Totally out of patience, William stood up and faced the minstrel squarely. "You," he said, leveling a finger at the youth, "seem to find yourself all too worthless. You don't seem to understand *who you are.* You are a good advisor, a superb musician, and, Orrin tells me, perhaps the smartest student he's ever encountered." The minstrel looked utterly shocked. "You find out information with little seeming effort and use it to head off various crises. You do two or three jobs with ease and still find time to plan a grand ball—and you manage to keep the rumors of such down until the tasks are well away. Melinda tells me you also act as a sort of counselor to the servants. And yet—" he looked at the ceiling in frustration, "and yet you still, after all that, think that you're somehow worthless.

Lord above, Alan, you're my friend. Who told you, all your life, that you were nothing, that you still think it's true?"

"Nobody told me," the minstrel replied, a little bitterly. "I *found out*." He swallowed and looked over the king's shoulder. "I found out what I was worth when... Lady be merciful..." the minstrel paused. "Smart? I can't be smart. How smart can a person be, to travel alone?" William was alarmed. Alan's eyes had gone wide with memory, and he wasn't looking at the king. He held his breath. Traveling was not, in itself, particularly dangerous, but for one who might be seen as an easy victim... that would explain a lot, actually.

While the king might be as casually unaware of the perils of poverty as any other young noble raised to privilege, he was not without an imagination, nor had Melinda let him get away with certain assumptions. The result was that he had a better idea of the dangers a solitary traveler might face than did most of his court. And though his messengers traveled alone, they were well-trained to defend themselves.

Unlike, William realized glumly, a noble lad who might be filled with tales of daring.

If only the minstrel would talk, and let the poison out of the memory. Alan looked up at him, and focused on his face. William was, for a moment, afraid that the recognition would close the minstrel off again. But the minstrel's gaze hardened. He knew that the minstrel was steeling himself.

"If I were smart, I would not have thought that a journey could be undertaken with no more concern than... than a morning walk. That there were no dangers other than distance and the cold. To some people, your worth is no more than the goods you bear."

"You were robbed?" William asked quietly. That would certainly account for the minstrel's apparent poverty. But Alan shook his head.

"He would have killed me, eventually, I think," he whispered. William's gorge rose at the possibilities that presented themselves with that quiet statement, and the next one took him quite by surprise. "I killed him, instead." The minstrel sat down, almost gently. He looked up at the king with an astonishing vulnerability, and no sign that he was going to go on.

In fact, he looked resigned to accept any action the king chose to take. He expected the worst. William was almost angry, that Alan could only expect that he would—what? Be dragged off to the dungeons as a murderer? Small doubt that Alan thought so little of himself.

And yet, he trusted the king to do the right thing. For all his apparent disdain of fireside tales, they'd marked him deeply; he trusted in his king. Melinda was right. William didn't know what he'd done to deserve such trust from his Minstrel.

"Did he hit you?" he probed, lowly. At the minstrel's surprised nod, he went on. "Did he hold you down? Did he take anything of yours?" At each confirming nod, William felt his ire rise a little. "How did he hold you down?"

Alan, confused, brought one hand up to his throat. William felt a surge of anger, quickly suppressed it, and wondered if this were the reason the minstrel wouldn't sing. Then William asked the hard question. "How did you kill him?"

The minstrel made an aborted motion, grasping off to the side, before clearing his throat and murmuring, "A knife, my lord. In the throat. I'd meant..." He shook his head again, refusing to defend himself. William could guess, though. It had been an accident and he'd paid for it with months or more of nightmares.

"Lady be merciful," he breathed fervently. "That's self-defense."

"I *know* that," Alan whispered. He was still looking at the floor; his arms, perhaps unconsciously, sought his shoulders, and he clutched at them in a pathetic imitation of prayer. William shook his head, confronted with a pain he did not understand. The minstrel, so ruthlessly practical in matters of the court, seemed utterly lost when it came to take matters, as it were, into his own hands. The king slumped into a chair.

"If you know that, then why did you bring it up?" Alan's face was shadowed by his hair. William bit his lip and continued, "It's as though you want me to think the worst of you." He sensed, rather than saw, the minstrel's flinch. The king closed his eyes and sent up a prayer. He'd hit a nerve, and after all these months... "Well then. Are you then trying to hurt *me?*"

Alan's face snapped up. "*No,*" he burst out. William nodded. Evidently that was the right track to take. "I trust you, Alan," he said gently.

"You shouldn't," came the reply, a little less anguished.

"I do."

"You..." The minstrel put his face in his folded hands and breathed deep, then let his hands drop. The look he gave the king was slightly embarrassed, as though he had just managed to trip and fall on his face in front of a room full of diplomats. William wondered, suddenly, what Alan's friends had thought of him. *Did he have any friends?*

"How did we get *on* this topic?" he asked, rhetorically. One expression after another chased itself across the minstrel's face. William smiled, a bit sadly, at the minstrel. "Sooner or later, you know, we will convince you that you're worthwhile."

That earned the ghost of a smile in return. William sent him off, well aware that Alan would need to have a chance to think things through. As he reviewed the conversation, he allowed himself to feel the anger that he'd suppressed for fear the minstrel would think it was directed toward *him*. He could well imagine the scene—a large man, or at any rate one larger and stronger than the minstrel-- assaulting a helpless boy on the road. And as for worse... well, it hadn't happened, as far as he could tell.

He frowned. For a moment, while Alan was talking, he'd gotten the impression that he'd seen him before, perhaps when he was younger. But the elusive sense of identity stayed out of his grasp. Ah, well. If it were important, it would resurface.

And with a sense of duty, he sat down to think of what he really wanted in a wife.

* * *

Lydia found herself in a corner of the kitchens, trembling. She had lost control *again*. She had never meant to let on about that man in the woods, yet it had just tumbled out of her mouth. Lydia twisted her lips. It was hard to keep secrets from William—from *the king*, she reminded herself firmly. If she started thinking of him as William, she'd be lost for certain.

He was under the impression that she thought herself worthless. She smothered a laugh. The moment her true identity was revealed, any worth she had built up for herself as Alan, King's Minstrel, would be thrown out in favor of the worth of Lydia, who was the wayward sister of the traitor, Richard Kentwell. And she knew that value. Lydia was worth more dead— even to her—than alive.

Perhaps she would tell him after he was married. She bit her lip. It would never do to let him know otherwise.

And then? Even her imagination failed her at that point.

Suddenly, Marta loomed over her, holding a large basket of jewelfruit from up north, their woody brown-red skins cracked to show rows of glistening garnet seeds. "No moping," she said concisely, and placed the basket on the table in front of the girl, pulling two large bowls over. "Seed these."

Lydia nodded, and pulled out one of the fruit. She'd done minor tasks for the cooks before, when sitting idle. Her agile fingers were well-suited to dealing with the fragile seeds. She used a small, claw-shaped knife to score the sides of the jewelfruit, breaking it into sections over a bowl.

Marta was wise, in her way. The trick of putting just the right pressure on the rows of seeds was oddly soothing. It kept her just distracted enough to keep her from obsessing over her thoughts, yet she still had the leisure to think on things.

The conclusions she came to were rather surprising. She hadn't thought of herself as particularly smart—though she hadn't thought of herself as particularly dumb, either. Was it just her love of reading? Was it just that the things that she thought were obvious were not?

She almost laughed. So smart, and she still couldn't figure herself out. *Don't lie to yourself, Lydia*—her revelation that afternoon had been an attempt to keep him from getting too close to her, because she didn't want him to mourn too badly when something happened to her. Or, and she sighed, she did want him to mourn, but nothing like the depression he'd felt when Lydia—dammit, that was her—had died. In a weird way, he'd mourned her once. He didn't need to do it again.

She paused with her hand over the basket of jewelfruit. When had she become convinced that something was going to happen to her? She hadn't used to be so fatalistic. She resolutely grabbed another fruit and held it over the bowl.

Only to shriek and fling it from her as something moved under her fingers.

The cooks went into hysterics, laughing at the expression on the minstrel's face. Lydia looked at the pomegranate on the table, and the brown-black segmented thing that had been hiding in the recesses of the fruit. Then she looked back up at the gaggle of laughing cooks. Paige wasn't laughing. Instead, she looked rather thoughtful, and Lydia realized that one more person, at least, had guessed she was a girl.

Resolutely, she picked up the fruit again, checking it carefully for any further surprises, and subsequently ignored the rest of the room with a flush in her cheeks.

*　　*　　*

Lydia examined the bristling target with a certain wry dismay. She'd been about this archery training for months, and yet the target could have almost been from her early days. While the arrows did, in fact, all hit the target, the matter of whether they hit the blot or not seemed to be a matter of luck rather than skill. With a sigh, she started pulling the arrows out again.

"I'll never make an archer," she observed, and was startled to hear a dry chuckle behind her. She turned to see the yardmaster, hands on hips.

"That isn't the point, minstrel," Martin said. "It takes years to make a good archer."

Lydia straightened up. "Then what *is* the goal?" She gestured at the arrows. "This target hasn't done anything offensive, and it seems a waste to fill it with arrows for no good cause."

The yardmaster walked over. Not for the first time, Lydia was struck by the assurance in his very walk. He didn't float across the ground as a noble lady would, but his feet were placed with utter surety. He was always balanced. "You're not a natural," Martin said, "but archery is good to train the eye and the mind, and it is good for strength. You're using a much stronger bow than you were this spring; it's hardly surprising that your aim should suffer." He held out his arm, and Lydia pulled down on it. Suddenly, he raised it and she found herself a few inches off the ground, arms still bent.

With a start, Lydia realized that the descent she'd made from the keep tower, those many months ago, would no longer be difficult to her. That breathless night seemed safely possible all of a sudden.

Martin lowered her again. "You are a lot stronger, and I should not be afraid for you if there were a fight." He grabbed her wrist and she twisted it free. Next, he moved to grab her and she ducked, sprinting over to her bow, where she stood, holding an arrow to the string. The yardmaster smiled broadly.

"And though you may not be able to hit a moving target, it is not likely that an attacker would know that." Once again, he planted his hands on his hips. "Besides, an arrow flying through the air makes a rather effective distraction." He stepped toward her. "But …you do have to make sure, that you *will* attack if it becomes necessary. All the defensive tricks in the world won't save you against someone determined to kill you."

Martin went on, "Even if you are afraid; even if it conjures up bad memories, and even if you have to use a knife…," he stopped right in front of her. Then, he pointed at her belt with the empty sheath, "…you will need to start carrying one again, lest people see you as too easy a target."

Lydia swallowed. "There is *no* such thing as a secret in this place," she protested.

The yardmaster grinned in the face of her obvious discomfort. "Oh, I think there are still plenty enough to go around. Think on what I said. You have to figure out, in your mind, what you will do *before* any situation comes up. You can't stay hidden within these walls forever, minstrel." Then he walked out of the yard, whistling faintly.

*   *   *

William watched, out of the corner of his eye, as the page passed on his message. The minstrel nodded, and returned his attention to the musicians in the gallery. To the king's surprise, he took up his harp and joined them on the next song.

Add musical training to the lists of things Alan somehow found time to do. Between practices with groups and teaching himself to pipe, he must be extraordinarily busy.

The king lingered after dinner until the hall was all but empty of the nobles. As requested, the minstrel came up to William and gave an utterly precise bow. "Your majesty wished to speak with me?" he said, lightly.

For a moment, the king was tempted to give the traditional response of "William," but a quick glance around the hall, with its pockets of chattering courtiers, decided him in favor of caution. "Walk with me, Minstrel; I should like to discuss the upcoming ball."

"Of course, sire," was the quiet reply. Alan's manner was utterly correct, so much so, that William was slightly worried. He asked several pertinent questions on the way to his study, to which the minstrel gave perfectly reasonable, but distant, replies.

Alan bowed to the king when they got to the study, indicating that William should precede him, and when the door shut behind them, he leaned against it with an exhaled breath. "Did I do it properly?" he asked, still propped against the door.

"Do *what* properly?" asked William.

"Act meek and subservient, as befits a grateful servitor whose position is surely the result of a charitable impulse," Alan recited, eyes closed. William, who had just been about to ask why the minstrel had avoided their morning meetings for the last several days, was speechless. Then, he recognized the tone of voice as one Alan used to pass on quotes.

"Who in the world is the idiot who told you that?" he asked, exasperated. It was no good to tell the minstrel of his value if nobles were going to undo all of his work the moment they got Alan alone.

Alan opened his eyes and essayed a smile. "No one, really, I just thought it was worth a try." He pushed off the door with the flats of his hands and leaned on the back of a chair. "There are going to be a few at the ball who will wonder at my marks of favor. It ought to be interesting to see what they do about it."

William blinked a few times. "Do you ever start a conversation in the normal way?"

The minstrel raised his eyebrows. "Why bother?" He gave an impish smile that looked a bit strained.

"I was worried about you, you know. You've been avoiding me."

Alan opened his mouth, closed it, shook his head, and spun the chair around, straddling it. "I have. But... it's because I needed to think." He sighed and rested his chin on his crossed arms. "It isn't really fair to ask you to exorcise your demons and then refuse to take my own advice."

"Demons?" William asked, amused.

Alan's smile looked less strained. "Well, I wouldn't precisely term the lingering effects of infatuation, a demon, but you were certainly acting half-ready to slip into a fashionable despair. And I..." He frowned. "I used to think I was happy, but I don't think I understood what happiness was." Alan's expression was rueful.

"What happened?" William breathed.

Alan gave him a serious look. "My fruit of happiness was poisoned. It's only luck that I discovered that before I ate it."

"And ran away."

"And ran away," the minstrel agreed.

"You *are* highborn."

The minstrel nodded. "I don't see any reason to deny it. There's no one to matter or to miss me." He said it lightly, but William found the whole concept utterly sad. Alan's sorry excuse for a family had obviously not known his worth either.

"Well, at least that's not true anymore," the king replied after a moment. In an attempt to lighten the tone of the conversation, William said, "Master Orrin, for one, would be dismayed to lose his prodigy."

He received a smile in return. "Yardmaster Martin would lose his chastiser of targets," replied the minstrel quietly. William pictured Alan haranguing the painted wood, and was hard pressed to keep his expression calm.

"Melinda would have to deal with substandard musicians on her own," he retorted.

"Maisry would have to find somebody else to mother," returned the minstrel. "Or big-sister, or something. She's younger than me," he went on, apropos of nothing. "I never had a sister."

The king was momentarily distracted. "Really? What..." He shook his head. "No, that's right, I wasn't to ask."

"Thank you," was the quiet reply. Alan sounded weary, as well he might be, but there was a strange pleading in his voice.

"If I were to tell you to sing," William said suddenly, "would you do it?"

Alan's look held the helpless certainty that he would, but he replied, "I will make you a promise if you won't command me to sing."

The king swallowed. "What promise is that?"

"I will sing at your wedding feast," the minstrel promised, "And you will wish I hadn't."

"A promise, then?"

"A promise," affirmed the minstrel.

" Still friends?"

The minstrel looked surprised. "Of course." The mercurial youth left, with a bow that was grace itself.

*　　*　　*

Lydia never quite remembered how she got to the hall again, only that she had kept her composure. The hall itself was dark, with moonlight providing barely enough light to see by. It was plenty enough for concealment.

Lydia walked to the alcove, placed one hand on her harp and suddenly sat on the bench, breathing hard. She shrank into the shadows, hiding her face, and tried to keep her breathing even.

She felt that she was treading a narrow precipice, one that took all of her concentration. She hadn't intended to be so open—she never did. It was as though the moment he asked her something, it was all she could do to keep her tongue from running free.

What was worse, a dishonest truth or an honest lie? There were certainly those who would be interested to find her yet alive. But to say as much would be to condemn her.

Only a few more weeks, she told herself. *Surely among all of the ladies we've invited there will be one that will be right for him. One who will be safe.*

Oh, Lord of Song, she'd promised to sing for him. What then?

Lydia gathered her resolve and her harp and began the trek back to her room. Well, she'd sing a verse or two in her little-girl soprano, giving everything away, and then... she could sneak out the back while the court was in confusion, and leave. With a little preparation, she could have everything ready to go. Perhaps she could go see the ambassador, or the southern duchies. Maybe she could travel with Eri, Tem, and Jessen.

She snorted. *Oh, yes, very dramatic.* Just like a story—sing a farewell, and disappear, leaving everybody to figure out what had happened. Almost as silly as escaping a tower on a rope made out of bedcurtains and sheets. Some days, she couldn't believe she'd actually done that.

Lydia closed her door softly behind her. She placed her harp on the table, and sat down on her bed with a sigh. *Oh, Lady of Truth, give me strength.*

Give me the strength to lie just a little while longer.

*   *   *

"Heya. Wake up!"

Lydia roused to a hand on her shoulder, and she sat up, blinking in confusion. The room was too bright, sun angled to midday, but Maisry didn't appear to be particularly worried. Lydia noticed, groggily, that she was still in her livery. She could remember arriving at her room after—what? Was it the pastry deliveries, or the banners?

She didn't remember sitting down, much less falling asleep.

Maisry was smiling at her as she blinked her way to the conclusion that she was running herself ragged over this ball. *Just a few more days...*

"Melinda's taking over now, minstrel," Maisry stated flat-out. "She told me to tell you that the thing is planned and there's nothing to be done that you need to do. *Then* she said there's nothing left to be done that she couldn't do better anyway, and I was not to mention that."

"Oh," Lydia replied vaguely. She really didn't feel awake yet. The maid was still standing there, shifting from foot to foot. "What is it, Maisry?"

"I wanted to show you something," Maisry said, and brought something from behind her back. Lydia took it gently.

It was a doll, a simple cloth doll with the merest suggestion of hands and feet, but which was clothed in the most exquisite tiny ballgown that Lydia had ever seen. Delicate, miniature lace that was threaded with ribbons trimmed the embroidered skirt and bodice. Panels of satin showed through slashes in the skirt and sleeves. The overall effect, which might have been overwhelming, was kept barely in check by the simplicity of line and form.

Lydia turned it over in her hands, marveling at the invisible stitching and colors. "Maisry, this is lovely." She looked up at the maid, more alert. "Did you make this?" There was a little color in the maid's cheeks as she nodded. Lydia smiled. "You want to be a draper, don't you."

Maisry bit her lip, then smiled. "I can't be a maid forever. Well, some can, but I want to sew."

Lydia nodded gravely. "And you'd like me to find you a place, wouldn't you."

"There's going to be so many ladies at this ball, there's sure to be one that could use a good draper."

"I can do better than that, Maisry. I'll find you one who sets the fashion, and recommend you to her." Lydia thought a moment. "If she's worth anything, that is." She looked at Maisry soberly. "There are some places I wouldn't send you for the world."

"Well..." drawled the maid, "If you can, I would like to stay here."

Lydia nodded, unsurprised. "To serve the new queen? That's not a bad idea either." She deliberately did not mention a certain guard.

"It could be you," Maisry replied.

Lydia stared for a minute. Suddenly, she burst out laughing. "Me? It's kind of you to say so, but I hardly think I'm going to be setting the fashion. Certainly not in gowns."

"We could dress you up for the ball," Maisry went on, quietly.

Lydia arched an eyebrow. "I am hardly Goldeneyes. First of all, this isn't a masquerade. Secondly, I'm already going as the Minstrel. I can hardly be in two places at once. *Lastly*," she said, cutting off the maid, "it would run exactly counter to what I'm trying to do! W— the king doesn't need any confusion right now!"

"No, you're not Goldeneyes," Maisry retorted, "though you do have the eyes. She was a scullery maid and you're highborn." She paused to see if Lydia would deny it, but the minstrel waved her on. "I don't see what your problem is."

"I am the *last* person he should marry," Lydia muttered. Raising her voice, she went on, "Wouldn't that be a joke, the king marrying a girl he found on the street? *And* thought was a boy, to boot? What a mess that would be."

"That's not it, is it," Maisry mused, hands on her hips. Lydia, in return, folded her arms and put the most stubborn look on her face that she could imagine. While she didn't want to lie to the maid, she didn't have to give her the truth, either.

Maisry crumbled first, but the look in her eyes confirmed what Lydia had known for the entire summer. It was only a matter of time before her secret was out, and Maisry could afford to be gracious.

*   *   *

William straightened his collar and took a lasting look in the mirror. His doublet was crimson, and closely embroidered with gold thread. He'd chosen a ruby ear-drop that swung near the angle of his jaw, and his circlet was likewise set with a ruby. All in all, he hoped he didn't look too intimidatingly royal, or he'd never get a dance at all.

What surprised him is that he actually looked as young as he did. Since the winter, he'd felt as though he were fifty, not the year or two that he had on the minstrel. An ancient thing, withered with care, not a youthful king holding his first ball. He grinned, and glanced over as the minstrel entered the room.

Someone had spent some effort on Alan's outfit as well; the fit was different than the anonymous livery, and cut closer. Curiously, the slimmer fit did not make Alan look nearly as waifish as the looser tunic, and the midnight fabric with silver embroidery rather flattered his coloring. His dancing shoes were made to coordinate, and somewhere in the stores, someone had found a pair of agate brooches that were a close match for his eye coloring. One hung at his neck while the other pinned a small fall of feathers to his hat.

Alan had declined the loan of an ear drop, and to look at him now, he had been right to do so. The overall effect was perfect, and tastefully restrained.

William waved him over, and turned him toward the mirror. The minstrel stared.

"What think you, to whom mirrors are a mystery?" the king asked, whimsically.

"I see the Sunrise King," breathed the minstrel. William glanced at his own outfit of red and gold, and replied, "You make the perfect foil as the Midnight Prince, an end to the day and to the story. I did not realize this was a masquerade."

"It is ever so," Alan said, absently. He leaned forward, looking closely at his own face. "Is that what I look like?" he asked, not quite rhetorically. "My eyes... I thought they were gray." He rubbed flat palms down the front of his legs.

"Are you nervous?" asked the king, surprised.

The minstrel swallowed, turned toward him, and smiled awkwardly. "I have never been to a ball before," he explained.

William stared. "Do you mean to say that you planned this all out without ever having been to one?" Alan nodded. "I thought you knew how to dance."

"I've had lessons," Alan said, apologetically. "But never... not with so many people. I didn't plan this part," he said, waving a hand at his elaborate outfit. "The rest is just asking, and planning." He clamped his mouth closed firmly, reining in his chattering tongue.

After a long moment, the king relented. "Shall we go, then?" Alan nodded, then bowed flamboyantly. As they walked through the corridor, William saw his manner change, as though the minstrel used extravagance as armor. Perhaps he did.

At the door, they paused. Then the minstrel slipped into the hall. William entered to the sound of the herald: "His Majesty, William VI of the house of Hawthorne, Guardian of Ellidar and King of Rooke!" The assembly, led by Minstrel Alan, bowed.

The candles in the hall were backed by tiny faceted mirrors, multiplying their light tenfold; such devices must have been hiding in storage. To compensate for the extra heat of the candles and lanterns, the doors and windows had been opened, but they had been blocked by free-standing screens so that breezes might not wreak havoc with the lighting. Panels likewise screened the various alcoves around the hall, and the lighting therein was dimmer, more calming, so that an overstimulated imagination might have some rest.

Or perhaps the fact that all of the young nobles he saw were as unmarried as the ladies might point to another reason for the half-secluded niches. William allowed his grin to escape. Alan couldn't have resisted the chance to play matchmaker to half the kingdom, not if he could do so for the king.

As the assembly rose, William wondered for an instant if he were supposed to say something, but the Minstrel nodded at the brightly lit gallery and the musicians began. He turned, almost at random, to the first nearby lady to offer a dance, and she, with a gracious smile, accepted.

He couldn't help but think, several figures later, that Alan was right on several counts. He needed this ball. He could already feel the tension leaving his shoulders. Moreover, it was surprisingly easy to sort the ladies in dancing. Several had been shy, and tense, and looked away. Those he had gratefully let free to go elsewhere; one had happily begun to dance with a younger son of Westridge, and spoke with him where she had been silent in the face of the king. A few ladies were less shy, and one had even bantered with him. He'd had the happy thought of giving her name to a page to write down; if he had more luck, he might find himself with several ladies to remember and it would not do to forget which ones they were.

He obtained a glass of wine from a servitor and stood off to the side for a minute. Alan was easy to spot: his midnight tunic seemed a spot of evening sky in amongst the bright colors of the ball. The minstrel was involved in a pattern dance, one that advanced and retreated in turn. Traditionally, this dance required palms pressed flat together, but the king could see, squinting, that Alan and his partner had chosen the more difficult style where the palms were held apart a fraction, the dancers moving as though there were a sheet of glass between them. Alan's face was blank, set in concentration, and the lady's held a slightly vicious smile, as though she were involved in a competition that she meant to win.

William became aware of voices on the other side of the screen. "Do you mean, then," said an unfamiliar female voice, "to go after Eastoak? He's reputed to be a very devil."

"He is," replied a voice that, to William's astonishment, proved to be that of one of the "shy" ladies, "but I've talked with his people. I can sway them to me. He can have his hawks and his hounds, and if he doesn't care for his lands I can work them better than he. And I know how to jess him. Stick to your songbirds; I like a challenge."

There was silence for a moment, and then the first voice said, musingly, "I don't want this Minstrel. But I wouldn't mind if he broke his heart a little over me."

William choked on his wine, then moved away from the screen so they wouldn't hear him laughing. Alan had been right that noble daughters were not stupid. But *he* was right that the King's Minstrel should draw some eyes as well.

*   *   *

After the musicians had quit for the night, and various couples had taken walks in the moonlit gardens or gone to bed, William stood in the hall, still floating on the joys of the evening. He had, indeed, come across several ladies to whom it would not be a chore to be wed. He'd danced with many ladies who were excellently light on their feet, heard beautiful music played by superb musicians, and quite thoroughly enjoyed himself. He'd speak with those ladies over the next several weeks and, who knows? Perhaps he would be able to announce a choice of bride by harvest time.

One of the servants taking down the extra lanterns walked near him, smiled, and jerked his head towards one of the alcoves. William walked over and saw, in the shadows, the minstrel sitting, asleep, his cheek pressed against the wall and his hands lax in his lap.

The king smiled for a moment as he looked on his friend. Asleep, he looked so calm, so untroubled, so unlike the bundle of nerves he often was, or the witty youth he pretended to be to cover up his tension. He extended a hand to the youth's shoulder, shaking gently lest he startle him. "Heya. Wake up, Alan. You'll get a crick in your neck."

Alan inhaled deeply, and gently opened his eyes, smiling. "No golden slipper?" he asked without preamble.

William, in shock, was rooted to the spot. For a bare instant, he looked at Alan's face and he knew, he *knew* who Alan was. But the realization was carried off on the waves of wine and fatigue, and he stood there, blinking in astonishment, with only the rock-hard certainty that he'd figured it all out. *This explains everything*.

But what explained it was gone. He dropped his hand, disturbed for some reason beyond thought. "Not exactly," he replied slowly. As the minstrel looked up, inquiring, he added, "It is not so hard as I had feared." He backed up a pace, suddenly afraid to touch the youth. "You should go to bed. It is so late that it is early once again."

Too sleepy to be confused, Alan nodded. He levered himself up off the bench, and made his slow way out the door. The king watched him the whole way.

*   *   *

A sudden pounding on the door woke Lydia out of a confused dream of pursuit, with strange figures of pattern dances part of the stalk. For a moment she thought it was Maisry, and then she recalled that maids don't knock.

She'd gone to bed still half-dressed, in shirt and breeches, and hadn't even bothered to loosen the corset, so she merely ran one hand through her hair and opened the door to confront a page in bleary-eyed confusion. "What is it?"

"Make haste, make haste," said the page, bouncing. "A northern delegation's come and there's a welcome *right now!*"

"Right now?" asked Lydia. The page nodded, and looked as though he would drag her out of the door, half-dressed as she was. She backed away, and said, "I will be there directly," and closed the door in his face when he looked as though he would follow her. She heard him pause, then race away from the door, presumably to get someone else that was needed.

Lydia scrambled, dragged a comb through her tangled locks, then fumbled on her doublet and short hose. Then she had to comb her hair again, something she might have figured out had she been more awake, found shoes, worked them on, and hat. She grabbed her harp bare minutes after the page had left, though it felt much longer.

She was at the door of the throne room before she realized that in her haste, she'd put on the outfit of the previous night and not her livery. She flushed, but decided to live with the consequences rather than be late. She stopped, drew a deep breath, and entered the hall to find that, as late as she was, the delegation had not yet entered. The king, who looked a little worried, indicated a seat near the dais as she bowed. She took it gratefully, not noticing his scrutiny.

Perhaps had she not been so distracted she might have realized the danger. As it was, she was entirely taken by surprise when the herald announced, "Duchess Siona of Kentwell."

Even as her head jerked up, she knew it was the wrong thing to do. *Magicians and pickpockets both know the value of distraction.* The snap of her head was visible across the room, visible to the golden-haired lady dressed in a gown of brown and cream and dull red. Her father's wife. There was a pause with all of the weight of years of silence behind it, then the woman in the doorway rushed forward.

"Lydia!" she cried, into sudden, shocked stillness. "Merciful heavens, child, we thought you were dead!"

"*Sunny,*" Lydia breathed.

Black as Coal, Red as Blood

The elder burned to see them free
Rosemary thistle and thorn
O sister, take a walk with me,'
Alas that I was born.

She threw her from the rocky shore
Rosemary, thistle and thorn
And watched until she breathed no more
Alas that I was born.

The maiden's body floated far
Rosemary, thistle and thorn
A minstrel spied it on the bar
Alas that I was born.

Full sorrowful for beauty fair
Rosemary, thistle and thorn
Strung in his harp her golden hair
Alas that I was born.

William had been fairly amused to see the minstrel hurry in, late, dressed in the previous night's finery. Alan was not often out of composure, and it was well worth the teasing. Something nagged at him, though, and he couldn't help but frown a little.

The herald announced the arrival of the most beautiful woman he'd ever seen. Golden-haired and fair of face, indeed, as the song said. He'd barely noticed the movement out of the corner of his eye, but well he saw the shock spread across the golden lady's face. Shock and, perhaps, a touch of horror.

An instant later, he might have imagined it, as the lady rushed forward and said the words that startled them all. Everyone's eyes turned to the Minstrel, whose poleaxed look was the very image of the death of hope. Alan—no, *Lydia*—whispered something, an oath or a prayer, and then blinked. In an instant, William saw a mask slip across her features, and she stood, putting the harp to one side as though it were of no moment.

"Lady Siona," she said demurely. Her whole demeanor had changed, so subtly that only those who knew her could have seen it. In an instant, she became, recognizably, a lady. She was dressed as a man, yet she was uncontrovertibly feminine.

The most surprising thing was, William realized, that he was not, in fact, surprised. Some part of him had figured this out, last night or long ago, and accepted it, and now it felt as though this were something he'd always known. Alan, his Minstrel, who did not feel worthy of trust. Who had a secretive past. Who worried about being friends with the king, and what a wife would think of him.

There was a buzz across the court as the two women faced each other. A few ladies snickered. Some of their wiser companions stayed silent. After a long moment, the duchess seemed to recall herself, and turned toward the king. "Your majesty, I think that in light of this... surprising reunion, we should retire, the Lady Lydia and I, and return to the thrust of this visit later." She shot a sharp look at the girl, who ignored it.

"You have my leave," William said, formally. He couldn't have managed much else. The duchess sank into a graceful curtsey. Lydia's hand flew up, for all the world as though she were going into one of her extravagant bows, then she gave the ghost of a smile and turned the motion into a spreading of the arms, a substitute for the skirts she did not wear, and for a bare instant it was as though she wore them.

As they left the room, pandemonium exploded. Each courtier and visitor were trying to fathom what had just happened. In the center of it all, ignored, William sat on the dais with his thoughts running in circles.

This explains everything. Except, really, it didn't.

*　　*　　*

Lydia followed her stepmother through the palace, servants dogging at their heels. She was outwardly composed—her composure had come at such a price!—but inwardly, she sought for some explanation to give, some tale that would satisfy the questions that Siona was sure to have. Something with some leavening of truth, perhaps, but she could not, in good conscience, tell the full tale.

They entered the suite that had been set aside for the duchess. To Lydia's eyes, the rooms were enormous, and opulent; she had so long been content with little that such space seemed awkwardly large. The Lady Siona stopped halfway in the first room, and Lydia did as well. She clasped her hands behind her, then recalled herself and took a more feminine stance. The servants looked wide-eyed. Lydia did not recognize any of them. *Here it comes*, she thought as the lady turned.

Siona gave her a curious smile, and then said, simply, "You and your stories."

Lydia felt as though she'd been slapped. *Is she trying to make me angry?* Anger drained away from her in an instant, though, looking at that gently worried face, her father's wife trying ever so hard to look concerned.

She doesn't know.

The Lady Siona didn't have the first clue about what was happening. She didn't know why Lydia had run away. She might even be ignorant as to the means. She didn't realize that Lydia Kentwell had spent months as Alan, King's Minstrel. She might even think that Lydia had only lately dressed as a boy.

Most of all, however, she would not know why Lydia was no longer fond of the stories that had once been so central to her life. Or what had sent her into the night.

The duchess went on. "Did you ever think what we were going through? How your disappearance would reflect on us? And now," she made a face as though she had a bad taste in her mouth, "to find you dressed... thus." She looked at the rich fabric with distaste, as though it were rags. "You cannot have been thinking."

Oh, Sunny, I have been thinking. Far harder than you would ever believe or want. "Lady, what is thy will?" Lydia asked formally. It was childishly easy to slip into the roles they had always played. Siona need never know that Lydia's thought trended in other directions now.

Siona frowned as she looked over Lydia's garments. "You will need to change. You cannot win the king through looking like a boy," she said. Her mouth twitched as though she would like to go on, but she refrained.

Lydia looked at Siona's gown, the beautiful gown that so flattered her coloring, and realized, for the first time, how young her stepmother truly was. She could hardly be seven years older than Lydia herself. She wondered, idly, if the Lady Siona regretted her outburst in the hall. But Sunny had never been one to let a perceived advantage slip. *I shall have to apologize to Ambassador Liend,* she thought, studying the face across from her. *I have wronged him.*

If I ever see him again.

They were both startled by a knock at the door, which one of the maids answered. She was confronted by some of the palace servants, bearing clothing and a great chest. One maid—Maisry—curtseyed to Siona and mumbled, "The Lady Lydia's clothes, your Grace."

Siona nodded tightly, and the servants herded Lydia towards one of the bedchambers and shut the door.

Once inside, she was impersonally stripped and given undergarments of silk. Maisry had an odd, half-worried smile; she took the special corset and folded it neatly, placing it beneath the doublet and breeches. She looked at Lydia in her shift and sat her down, combing her hair. The door opened as the other servants left, revealing Lindy, who exchanged glances with Maisry. The maid put a finger to her lips, indicating possible listeners, and Lindy nodded. In her usual collection of far too many items, she had a stoppered bottle and a basin. She motioned to Lydia that she was to wash her hair.

The liquid in the bottle was astringent, containing vinegar and unfamiliar herbs. When Lydia pulled a strand of hair in front of her eyes it was almost the color of polished copper, only slightly dimmed from the remnants of dye. "Close your eyes," Lindy murmured to her, and cleaned her eyebrows.

Maisry strapped her into a more normal corset, but only tightened it gently. Then, she unfolded a dream of dusky green and pale yellow. It was a dress that she might have intended for Lydia to wear to the ball. The maids helped her into it—Lydia, for a moment, longed for the sort of clothing one could put on by oneself—and Lindy finished by using combs to pull Lydia's short hair away from her face and attach a golden net lined with silk that mimicked the bundled fall of hair she no longer had. "Look," she said, and turned Lydia toward a mirror that hung behind the small table.

Lydia looked into golden eyes, pupils slightly mismatched, beneath fiery hair. The dress had completed the transformation; where before she had looked like a girl in boy's clothing, she now looked like a lady. Maisry watched from behind her, pleased with her work, and the maid leaned forward, just slightly, to whisper in Lydia's ear: "Are you in trouble?"

Equally quietly, Lydia replied, "I was born to trouble. I would not have you join me in it."

The maid looked sad, but complied. Lydia straightened up, turned, and went into the main room.

Siona looked up from the chair where she sat, writing. She seemed mildly surprised to see Lydia looking so well, and stood up. Lydia looked carefully at the beautiful, oh so flattering gown her stepmother wore. The gown might well dazzle a king, and Lydia knew that her own suited her as well, to the Lady Siona's dismay. Siona had, perhaps, thought to have the battlefield clear. She had not counted on the appearance of the king's lost love.

Lydia understood that though Siona knew she was a threat to her plans, she had no idea just how big a threat her stepdaughter truly was.

She looked into the face of her father's wife and smiled.

She was not afraid.

*   *   *

William looked carefully at the chair in front of him. It had been in the study all his life, perhaps longer; it had been there the day his father had first granted him the use of the room. Its arms were carefully carved, but when one studied it, one could tell that the left arm was not quite a mirror of the right, as though it had to be re-carved after some careless nick. The plump cushions had been re-upholstered a few years ago in a rich reddish brown and a needleworker had done some embroidery in an abstract pattern that reminded William of the fine details edging a spring jacket.

All of that, and it was just a chair. It was something to sit on, to walk around, and to get in the way. Furniture. If you'd asked him yesterday what color it was when he was not in the room, he would probably have failed to call it up. One never really noticed furniture. One accepted it, and paid attention to other things.

Strange how trying to avoid thinking about a subject meant thinking about it more.

A faint knock at the door, and Melinda entered the room. She took a look at the king sitting across from the empty chair, and her lips twisted.

"How long have you known?" William asked. Melinda did not take a seat, but stood off to the side, subdued. He had never seen her subdued.

"That she was a girl?" Melinda asked. "Shortly after she came. That she was Lydia?" She shook her head.

"I can't imagine why she never said anything."

Melinda's gaze grew sharp. "You can't? Lord above, highness, think for a moment. When did you bring her here?"

William looked up, considering. "At the end of winter, wasn't it? A few months after..." His face drained of color. "Sweet Lady of mercy."

Melinda nodded grimly. "A few months after young Richard Kentwell stirred up the western duchies and so spectacularly failed that midnight ambush, and was sentenced to die for his treachery. Her brother."

"Her *twin* brother." William realized something else, then.

William thought he'd been thoughtlessly cruel before; to have left a sensitive, hero-worshiping lad in the company of his false idol, and to hear treachery explained in thorough detail. Now, he realized that was, instead, grotesque—a loving sister, hoping for innocence, finding only the truth of the rumors from the unknowing source.

She hadn't revealed herself to Richard. Even now, he was sure of that. He'd asked for honesty, and in all things but one, she'd lived up to that pledge. But that one...

Lord and Lady both. He'd killed her brother. And sent her, in his blithe ignorance, to hear his last confession.

We were both the more deceived.

Melinda's expression was thoughtful as she watched him work this through. "I don't know yet why she ran away. I pray that she'll accept help if she needs it, but I fear that she will not."

William nodded. Whatever had happened, whatever she had run from, she had more than once displayed an unwillingness to get anyone else involved. Or, in any way, reveal herself as herself. He winced as he remembered her falling to the floor, beaten but somehow still focused on the king.

I loved her!

Did you? Did you even know her?

His memories mocked him. She'd hinted at the truth all along, and he hadn't the wit to see it. He looked up at Melinda, anguish on his features. "What are we to do?"

Melinda tightened her lips. "Well, to begin with, you can't go out looking like that, highness. This chance has happened in front of dozens of your most powerful nobility. *Alan* was very thorough with the guest list and you can be sure that some of them will be looking for advantage."

The king winced. "So what should I expect?"

"Rumors. Gossip. Slander. They'll try to use her circumstances against her—Lord knows, I've tried to laugh off where she was found, but that's bound to resurface. I don't *think* anyone but the servants and the guard knows that she would come up here of a morning but it only takes one careless word. They'll call her your 'whore', or worse."

William nodded dully. The best tactician and advisor he'd ever had and they'd drag her name through the mud before long. "What else?"

Melinda sighed. "I was hoping you could tell me." At his shaking head, she went on, "I'd hoped you had some insight as to why she ran away."

William thought back to his first talk with her. She'd seemed shocked at the idea of the Lady Lydia being used in schemes of power. He didn't know how that had affected her personality, but he was sure it had come as a surprise to her. *Which meant... what, exactly?* "I don't know."

Melinda folded her hands together. "Then, I suggest we should tread warily, your majesty. It is worrisome that we should have thought the lady dead when, in fact, she is not."

William considered this. Not missing, nor lost, but dead. *I find it convenient that she should die in such a manner.*

The minstrel's worries and fears loomed large in William's perception, as well as the insistence that the king should marry, and soon. *Why?* To protect him from Lydia? That made no sense. All the lady had to do was refuse to wed. To protect him from someone else?

William remembered the golden lady standing in the doorway. Pausing for an instant, he thought. *Who had sent word of Lydia's death, after all?* Of her funeral, too swift for Richard to return in the summer's heat? Could it be that lovely lady?

Or was she a pawn too, in someone else's scheme?

William laughed, bitterly. At Melinda's raised eyebrow, he said, "I was just thinking that this is exactly the sort of tangle Alan could unravel. But, he won't be planning any strategy here."

Melinda exhaled, slowly. "No. I am afraid that Alan is gone. But Lydia lives."

Lydia: *naïve, romantic, easily led*. Alan: canny, intelligent, and an absolute genius at seeing to the heart of things. It did not seem right to think of Lydia alive and Alan gone. It felt like mourning. And they would expect him to be overjoyed that his lost love yet lived, he supposed.

His smile was not so bitter this time. Alan was not gone, not so long as he could provide an example. If Lydia could confound them all for months, William could hardly fail to learn by her example.

"Melinda, attend me. I think I know what we shall do."

*   *   *

In the afternoon, he met with the Duchess. Only a few people were in the hall for this welcome, unlike the disastrous morning meeting: the Duchess, himself, and a few guards. He restrained his disappointment that she had not brought Lydia with her and listened carefully as she went through a formal request for aid. She wanted food to supplement a bad harvest through the winter. Duchess Siona faltered a bit when she spoke of the recompense she would offer, the service and goods that were required. Small doubt but that the appearance of a child thought long dead would rattle her a bit.

Alan predicted this, William thought with no small wonder. *Predicted that the drought would bring this very request, and sent Guardron to prepare for it.*

His thoughts took a small lurch as the disconnect between Alan and Lydia reasserted itself. *But if she knew this was coming, why did it surprise her so? And why is this lady here? Surely someone else in her employ could have managed it...*

He looked at the woman with new interest. She had come herself instead of sending a clerk or messenger. William realized that she was not much older than he was, and a widow. Unmarried.

He was utterly certain that she had not received an invitation to the ball, despite her arrival close on its heels. Whether this was due to fears on Lydia's part of a premature unveiling or of some deeper cause, the king had no idea. But he felt he could be certain that in either guise, the Minstrel did not want Lady Siona in the capitol.

In careful phrases he assured the Duchess of the swift response of the kingdom. She seemed a trifle disconcerted that an aid party could be sent in a matter of days, as soon as the messenger boat were sent to Guardron. She still looked thoughtful as she rose, as though she would have to rethink her plans.

We all do, was his thought.

*   *   *

As was only fit, the Duchess Siona was to be seated just to the left of the king for the dinner that night. William entered the hall to see the tables set thickly about the hall, scarcely leaving room for the servers to move in between them. Half of the tables were already filled and he felt a little ill at the excited buzz that attended his entry.

But he braced himself to act as though nothing extraordinary had happened. As though the morning's revelation were a minor annoyance. *Forgive me, Lydia*, he thought. Pretending that he scarcely knew her for anything beyond a dutiful servitor was the best protection he could offer. He wondered, suddenly, how much she had been acting at any given moment. Had she, too, been trying to protect *him* in the only way she knew?

The buzz increased when the Duchess and Lydia arrived. Siona was still beautiful in her cream-colored dress, but Lydia was stunning in a dress the color of summer oak leaves. Her hair had somehow been returned to its natural color, and her eyebrows as well—they were lighter, and finer, and it was amazing how such a little thing could change an appearance so much.

He tried not to stare. His nonchalance was strained as he gave formal greetings to both ladies, to Lydia as calmly as to the Duchess. Lydia had that not-quite smile on her face, something that usually hinted at a vast interior amusement.

William thought that if she started laughing, he would have no choice but to go into hysterics. The situation would be hilarious in many other circumstances. Here they were, two people intent on pretending they barely knew each other, all in order to stem malicious gossip that would continue apace regardless. In truth, if they didn't give the scandal-minded something, events would probably be made up.

And even so, he could read her expressions well, as though only the two of them knew how ridiculous the situation was.

When they sat to dinner, he very carefully made conversation with the Duchess, ruthlessly ignoring the girl who sat by her side. Lydia was quiet, answering questions from the gentleman to her left in the briefest manner possible, but as though she were shy, not rude. William thought of the long, witty, and utterly unself-conscious talks they had had, and addressed some comments towards the lady to his right.

With all of the confusion of the day, he hadn't thought to implement his list, and the Lady Nadya was less than a sparkling conversationalist, preferring to instead stare at Lydia in a constant astonishment. Lydia ignored it with an aplomb that belied her shy mannerisms.

The soup course was the sternest trial. Lydia went blank-faced as the servers put a bowl down in front of her that was patterned just the same as all of the other bowls, but which was half again as large as the others. She did not look up, nor smile, but William once again had to suppress hysteria as he engaged the Duchess Siona in conversation once more. He survived the final comfits and gracefully made an escape, no doubt disappointing those who had hoped for something to rival the morning's excitement.

He was out in the antechamber before he realized that there had been music playing for the entire dinner. William had not heard a single note.

*   *   *

Several days—long, infuriating, utterly pointless days—went on in this manner. Much to his surprise, William got a lot of work done. But then, he supposed, it was hardly surprising that he'd have plenty of time. He'd left his days open, thinking that he would be comparing notes with the Minstrel, or arranging times with whomever he might meet at the ball, or—if all went really well—speaking to parents or ministers, preparing documents.

Instead, he was left alone, all too alone, and to keep himself from going crazy he signed things that must be signed, or studied problems that were arising. One bit of information caught his attention briefly; it was a note on the situation in Erlein. It was just barely possible that there was advantage for the ambassador or his family in that situation, a thought that was almost soothing. Liend was a rather frightening person in his way, especially as he always seemed to know so much but tell so little, but William thought well of him for all that. It was reassuring that Liend should be so happy because of events at home, rather than secret treaties in Rooke.

Dinners were also maddening. Lydia was not always seated so near but William couldn't help but note where she was and the dual trials of pretending he barely knew her and controlling his own bleak humor at the situation meant that he wasn't eating very well. He had, however, gotten his list to Melinda, and his dinner conversation actually required enough concentration that a few times, he was actually diverted from his problems.

The Duchess of Kentwell also seemed subdued. There had been a few times, when they were fixing the details of how Kentwell would pay for its aid, that she would falter, as if wanting to change the subject.. William, with grim amusement, thought she might be trying to bring up Lydia, and didn't know quite how to phrase it. He was not going to introduce that idea himself, and so acted in a businesslike manner, as though nothing could be further from his mind than getting the details correct.

In the end, though, he had done his work too well. Five days after the ball, he looked down at a desk that was clear of paper and parchment both. He looked at the morning ahead of him, which was empty of appointments. He started poking around in the drawers, hoping for something to distract him. His fingers closed on a bundle of papers that didn't match—they felt different, cut shorter, and were of a softer texture.

What he pulled out was something he had forgotten completely. The music in his hand had never been reclaimed by the Minstrel, a song that he—she—had perhaps forgotten about. William flattened the sheets absently, looking at the arrangement of dots and lines as though they could mean something to him. He flipped through the pages, and saw one sentence fragment, no, two, written on the margin of the paper as though they went with the music.

"Let me share your dream for a while," said one, and, "We, unhearing, dare to dream, and hope for nothing more."

William puzzled over the phrases for a bit. They weren't poetry, quite, and they didn't seem like any lyrics he knew. The second—ah, the second was rather sad, in a way. What had happened to her, so that she was afraid to hope? And this talk of dreams and dreaming? She had nightmares, she had said as much.

Nightmares where she caused the death of the king. William swallowed. As often as she'd railed at him about feeling too much guilt over things that he did not control, he wasn't sure he would ever not feel guilty over Richard. Over sending her to watch over his last night. It didn't take a genius to figure out where such dreams might come from.

William blinked, and looked out the window, not really seeing the familiar view. What did she dream now, back with a family that cared so little for her that she had left them behind without a second thought? His attention was caught by movement in the gardens below. He stood and walked over to the window, leaning against the edge.

It was Lydia, of course. She walked through the gardens, never looking up, in a dress of mossy green. Close at hand was a guard with the wheat sheaf badge of Kentwell on his shoulder. William wondered, dully, if she had been doing this for days in the hopes that he might look down and see her, but she never looked up. He almost hammered on the glass in frustration but thought better of it. There was the guard, after all.

After a moment, she took hold of a rose that was still in bloom despite the lateness of the season. She took a small knife from her belt and severed it from the bush, then idly started snapping the thorns off the stem. She was mostly turned away from the window; William could barely see movement as her fingers worked. This wasn't some sort of message, was it? She couldn't know he was watching.

Two other ladies and their attendants rounded a hedge. One of them smirked and said something to Lydia, who looked up. William couldn't see her face but he could imagine the level tone of her reply, especially as the smirking girl frowned and said something else, her mouth twisting. Lydia extended her rose, placing it gently in the lady's outstretched hand and folding her fingers around the stem. The gesture was obviously unappreciated; the other lady held her companion back as she jerked forward, rose dropped to the ground.

The guard said something; Lydia waved a hand in an oddly sinuous movement, dismissing the encounter as she turned and walked away. William caught only a glance of her face, tight at the lips, before she passed out of sight.

*   *   *

A few hours later, there was a knock at the study door, and a page darted in. This one was new, and quite visibly nervous as he stammered through the news that the Duchess of Kentwell would like to attend him in his study. He also seemed more than a little disconcerted to find the king sitting on the deep windowsill, one knee drawn up.

William mentally rolled his eyes up, thinking that he should speak to Orrin about his training program. It usually took several months to calm a page down after the Protocol Master first got ahold of him. Their meticulously correct attitude was more than a little maddening.

When the Duchess Siona entered, William was more properly sitting in his chair. He did not sit up any straighter when Lydia entered, demurely pacing behind the Duchess. For a moment, however, his breath caught short as he tried to figure out what was meant by this. Both ladies made graceful curtseys, the Duchess Siona taking a seat across from the king, while Lydia sat behind her, in an armless chair.

"Your majesty," the Lady Siona began, "the speed at which you have honored Kentwell's request is most gratifying. None of my party had any such idea that negotiations could be concluded so quickly." Lydia shifted in her chair and the Duchess frowned, briefly. "Lydia, dear, would you play for us, perhaps? I know that you are bored at this business." As her back was turned, Siona did not see William's eyes widen at this total misapprehension of Lydia's character.

"Of course, Lady Siona," Lydia murmured. She stood and went to the door, speaking quietly to the page outside, before she returned to her seat. She glanced over at his desk and her lips quirked as she took note of its empty state.

Siona went on, "As our business is concluding so speedily, we have an opportunity I had not thought possible. If we leave soon, we should be able to return home before storms close the Flamegold Pass." William looked his surprise; it was barely harvest. "Your majesty, I would not impose on you longer than is necessary."

William thought her tone indicated rather the reverse; perhaps she had been hoping to be present for the entire winter court, trapped by storms south of the mountains. He could see, out of the corner of his eye, a rather fey smile on Lydia's face. She returned to the door when a timid rap sounded and came back bearing her harp. Without hesitation, she began to play. The Duchess noted the unconscious smile that William could not suppress.

"She plays well, does she not, highness? She would often play so for the family." William wrenched his attention back to the lady, suddenly afraid he had given something away. And Lydia wasn't playing that well, not truly; her harping was simple, almost children's exercises compared to the exhibitions she normally put on.

But as Siona continued speaking, finalizing the details of her visit, he realized that Lydia was deliberately playing so, in a style that might once have been hers, long ago. *Hiding, always hiding,* he thought. William wondered if he had ever known what she was.

It was a hard question to have to ask.

*   *   *

There were several more meetings with the Duchess, but Lydia had thought so far ahead that the plans were already in place. Within the week, it became obvious that the Duchess could not stall any longer, and she made ready to go. Lydia was to travel with her.

William could not understand. Lydia was free to stay, if she so desired; in the few glimpses he had caught, she had not seemed overjoyed to be returning to the home she had abandoned. He had not, however, managed to let her know that she could stay—because it would cause talk, Melinda said. As though there weren't enough stories going around regardless.

He'd managed to deflect most of it by smiling vaguely and looking confused every time he'd walked past suddenly quiet gossipers, as though what he'd overheard hadn't infuriated him. Melinda had been right; they'd called her a whore. They had said much worse. Oddly enough, the rumors didn't spill over to him much; while they excoriated the girl, they'd acted as though he were utterly blameless, which was amusing in a twisted way.

It had taken every last ounce of his restraint not to put his fist in Eastoak's face; despite the fact that he had been there when "Alan" was found, the swaggering boor was spreading as much poison as he could about the erstwhile Minstrel.

William wondered, suddenly, what the Duchess Siona thought about the business, and how Lydia had explained herself. As far as he knew, no one had had the gall to repeat the rumors to Lydia... unless that confrontation in the garden had been one such repetition. He dearly wished he could compare stories with her, but he hadn't dared.

He realized that his presence in the courtyard, as the Kentwell delegation saddled up, would probably not meet with her approval. He watched as Lydia mounted a bay mare with the assistance of a stableboy, assistance she looked on the verge of spurning until she recalled herself. Her split skirts were a sensible russet, and she smoothed the mare's neck with that odd, fey smile.

William swallowed as the leaders of the party started out the gate. Lydia hung back, fussing, and he took the opportunity to walk up to her.

"Your majesty," she murmured, still bent over the mare's neck. "Is she not fine? She was a gift to me, two years ago. I had not thought they should bring her."

For a moment, it was as though she really were a stranger. William glanced around and saw no one within earshot. "You once promised to tell me the truth," he said quietly. She sat up straighter. The distant smile looked a bit strained, but her eyes spoke volumes as she looked just past his shoulder.

"I did," she replied quietly, and smiled. "I have, as I could."

William's mouth worked for a minute, and then he blurted, "Did Lydia ever love me?" He winced at the phrasing.

For a moment, her expression crumbled into pain. "Oh..."

Behind her, a guardsman rode up. "Milady?"

Lydia closed her eyes. When she opened them, the mask was back in place, a placid show for any who might be watching. "Fare you well, your majesty," she said lightly, as though she were the stranger that she pretended to be. Then she meekly followed the guard out of the courtyard, while the king watched her leave, more distant to him than when she had been thought dead.

William fought to control his expression. To his surprise, Orrin, the Protocol Master, walked over from the other side of the courtyard. He supposed that should not be so remarkable; Orrin did leave his rooms from time to time, and Lydia had been a special protégé of his.

"She will make an excellent Duchess, your majesty," he began without preamble. William stared at him for a moment.

"Duchess?" he finally managed.

The elegant eyebrows rose in surprise. "Have you forgotten your education so soon, then, sire? Her brother was Duke, and had no heir, so she is regent for her younger brother—and Duchess until he comes of age."

William frowned. "But the Lady Siona..." He could not finish the sentence. The Lady Siona had acted the Duchess, and Lydia had made no move to stop her or assert her rights, which she surely would have known.

William looked through the now-empty gate. "She never said a word," he mused. Orrin looked thoughtful.

What game was she playing now?

*   *   *

Riding a horse after so long out of the saddle was a strange sensation. On the one hand, the exercises and stretches she had been doing made her muscles far less sore than when she had first learned to ride.

On the other hand, her clothes still chafed.

Lydia found the sensation a welcome distraction from her thoughts. Plots, actually. She smiled a little at her hubris. Here she was, surrounded by Siona's guardsmen and attendants, and still trying to do more than she could. It had almost worked, back at the castle—William really had been amenable to getting married, amenable to forgetting that he had once imagined himself in true love.

Lydia tried to forget his face there at the end. It wasn't fair to him, really, but she hoped he would figure it out in time. She wondered what Guardron would think when he saw her. If he wasn't too shocked, she might be able to drop a hint to him. But, that would only happen if she made it that far.

She almost shuddered as she looked ahead and saw the strong back of the captain of the Kentwell guard. Martin had taught her well. Lydia now understood all too well why she was afraid and why she had to ruthlessly control her every look and action.

The man—his speculative looks, his flat uncaring gaze—was pure danger. Couldn't Siona see that? Didn't she see that here was a man who would, if it suited his interests, do anything up to and including murder?

Perhaps she knew. But Lydia wasn't certain that her unworldly stepmother noticed such things.

She hadn't seemed to notice the gossip that swirled around Lydia like leaves in an autumn breeze. But then, the Lady Siona did not encourage conversation. Nor did she listen to, what she irritatedly termed, "servant chatter." Lydia smiled sourly. If she had, she might have treated Lydia differently, not as a child.

Their progress toward the pass was surprisingly slow. Lydia had walked a similar distance in nearly the same time, but the horses were never pressed very hard, and they always stopped well before sundown. The first few days, Lydia had, in fact, been stiff when she descended from the saddle, but a little surreptitious stretching in her rooms after dark had quickly set that right. As they went further to the northwest, that stiffness eased and she was as fit for riding as she had ever been.

She stroked the mare's neck sadly. She was a fine mount indeed, and Richard had truly picked well when he bought her.

To her surprise, Lydia found herself taking as great or greater an interest in the countryside than she had when she first came south. The beginnings of autumn seemed almost heartbreakingly beautiful to one who did not expect to ever see this region again. She began going over her history lessons in her mind, finding a surprising number of battle sites were within view of the road.

Or perhaps that was not so surprising, after all.

They had stayed at inns every night thus far, so when they rode into the yard of one at the very base of the foothills Lydia was unsurprised. As she dismounted, she caught the sound of music coming from the open doorway and genuinely smiled for the first time in far too long. Then the song became clear to her.

She didn't give herself time to think, afraid that she might lose her chance. She quickly entered the inn's public room while the rest of the party was still fussing about the horses and strode right up to the musicians at the front, pulling some coins out of the small pouch at her belt.

"That's lovely," she said, smiling as she pressed the silver into the startled gittern player's hand. "Do you have any more new songs?"

"My... my lady?" replied Jessen, his eyes wide as he looked at his hand. Then he looked at her eyes and all color drained from his face. Behind him, Tem started to speak and was stopped by an elbow from his frowning sister. Lydia pressed on Jessen's hand, willing him to silence as she pleaded with her eyes.

The gitternist swallowed. "Yes, my lady, we do. Fit for..." he broke off, glancing at his partners. "Fit for the king."

Lydia nodded slowly. "Yes. Fit for the king," she repeated. Behind her, she heard a guard's measured approach. "Thank you," she whispered.

A hand touched her shoulder, and the guard said, "My lady. You should not be speaking with such..." he waved a hand at the trio. Lydia turned, as innocent as sunrise. "I shouldn't? Oh. But they play so well!"

The guard relaxed and led her back to her party and their private rooms. Lydia could feel the eyes of the trio and the few startled patrons on the back of her neck, speculating.

Let them speculate, as long as they understood. Jessen or Eri would probably figure it out.

*   *   *

Lydia's reappearance turned out to be a nine days' wonder; almost as soon as she had left, the gossip had died down to nothing. William alternated between relief that her name was no longer being dragged through the mud and anger that she should be forgotten so quickly and so easily. Within a fortnight, the bulk of the huge horde that had come for the ball had departed to return home before the onset of winter; not a few with new alliances being planned.

All for them, and not for the king, he thought somewhat whimsically. Whatever plans Alan had made for the king's marriage had fallen through in the light of the revelation that Lydia still lived. Lived, and for some reason, did not want to marry him. He didn't—precisely—think that she outright hated him— nobody could be that subtle of an actor, even in light of her seven-months' masquerade—but she was likely wary of him in light of the fact that he'd had to execute her brother.

He laughed dully at the thought. *Wary of him?* She should be wary of that acquisitive stepmother of hers.

William no longer bothered to pretend to himself. He missed Lydia desperately, and in her absence his sense of humor had taken a turn for the sardonic. He'd made more than one courtier wince with a bitter remark and he could only hope that his newly sarcastic tongue hadn't made too many enemies.

The worst part of it was that he didn't understand what she was doing. He didn't think she'd wanted to leave. All it would have taken was one word and she could have stayed.

To be fair, if she had stayed the rumors would have only gotten worse. And her comment, too often made, that he could not concentrate with the image of a dead love in front of him, still held all too true. The fact that she was still alive made little difference.

He had managed to remain civil, even attentive, to those ladies who had so lately been the focus of so many hopes. And there were two—one from Beechen, of all places, and one from Galeskeep—to whom it could be even pleasant to be wed. The latter, Rissa, might well have held his attention longer had it not been for Lydia. She'd been fairly gracious about the subject, commenting that he might be better company when he was not in shock, and offering to write regardless of how "his business" turned out.

But now the dinners were down to a reasonable size, and the servants didn't have to be dancers to dodge in between the tables. William knuckled his forehead. He had to stop his thoughts from going in circles. Lydia herself would object.

There was still a steady supply of musicians, even though the Minstrel was no longer in residence. Melinda had mentioned that when the contracted performers ran out, she was capable of screening the new hires. He looked up at the trio in the gallery; they looked familiar, but there had been so many in recent weeks, it could have been any of them.

The group at his table was fairly quiet that evening; he recognized at least one younger son who had gotten in his way when the king was in a foul mood. Instead of verbal gambits, that courtier only shot worried glances at the king. William shrugged. He was not precisely a sparkling conversationalist of late.

He noticed, during a pause in the music, what sounded like a suppressed argument. He turned to see the singer, hands on hips, hiss something at the gittern player, while the flautist tried to placate her. Whatever it was, it was momentary; the singer shrugged and turned back toward the hall, and only frowned briefly as the gitternist started on a set on unfamiliar chords.

The song itself did not seem to be a subject of such dissent, seeing as it was a lighthearted tale of a defiant girl faced with too many suitors. It might even be considered apt in light of the recent ball. William lifted his wine glass.

"And today's the day I wed, *Oh le-lay-o bah-i-a*," sang the dark-haired singer, "And tomorrow I'll be dead, *Oh le-lay-o bah-i-a*."

What would you do had I died?

William went numb, and put the wine down without tasting it. With a sort of dawning horror, he heard his own voice in memory, telling a beaten and bruised minstrel that if he had been a noble, the crown could investigate his death, investigate anything, even another noble. He heard, again and again, the worries of a minstrel who was sure that there was treachery, and worries without proof.

In such an investigation, any proof to be found would be found, if the death were of somebody noble. If *she* were noble.

William stood abruptly. The other diners looked at him with varying degrees of shock. He turned and left the hall without a word. By the time he reached his study, he was almost stumbling, blinded by the memories arising, all too late. All he could think was that she had set the perfect trap, a trap baited with the irresistible sacrifice. "You always undervalued yourself, Lydia," he whispered to memory.

The perfect snare. And she expected William to spring it.

"Ai, Lady, protect her," he whispered, and put his face in his hands.

Fool that he was, he'd asked her if she loved him.

*   *   *

They'd left the last inn at the foot of the pass. The guards had finally relaxed around Lydia and her harmless chatter, and she'd asked the innkeeper about the name of his inn, the Lucky Pinecone. He'd told her of the giant trees in the pass, found amongst the aspen. They were great circle pines that dropped pinecones of an unusual purplish hue. He'd also informed them that it was as hot in the pass as it ever got, so there was no worry of snow to impede their passage.

It was intriguing, Lydia thought, how even when she was certain that she would not survive for another year, her curiosity knew no bounds. There was no purpose to knowing of some obscure tree, found only at certain altitudes. And yet it made her smile to know its name.

There was actually a tent for her amongst the baggage. She was startled when it was set up—she had no objection to sleeping beneath the stars, but Siona could hardly know that. And she could not fathom why there was a second elaborate tent when Siona should only need one. Of course, Lydia realized, if anyone could find a need for a second tent, it was her propriety-driven stepmother.

The first night, Lydia lay awake, worrying over many things. Several of the attendants had split off, earlier, to take the lower, narrower Cedar Pass. The captain of the guard had actually volunteered the information that those attendants had been very ill with mountain sickness on the journey south and would take the difficult route rather than suffer such again. Remembering the journey she had made through that pass, Lydia shuddered—in places it was little more than a goat track, childishly easy for a person on foot but perilous to a rider.

What worried her more was the fact that in sending those people away, the group was considerably smaller—there were a bare handful of guards, only three of Siona's personal attendants, a few drovers and baggage handlers. Lydia understood that she was not meant to make it out of the mountains.

The next day's ride was difficult—Lydia nearly fell off her horse when the motion started to put her to sleep. She tried to concentrate on the vistas that started to open up, and take in the breathtaking views as they climbed higher and the valleys dropped away. By mid-morning, the road had changed from dirt to crumbled rock, and they still had two more days to climb before the long descent into Kentwell. She saw the splendid peak of Mithe Áne, standing alone amongst a stunning vista. It took her breath away at the sight. There was still a hint of snow at the top despite the dry summer. Soon, it was screened by nearer, smaller ridges, but the memory of that first glimpse sustained her for some time.

The silence of the ride dampened Lydia's spirits. The maids talked amongst themselves but would fall silent the moment Lydia would get near them; the guards took their duties very seriously and said not a word. The captain of the guard rode near to the Lady Siona, who made no speech the entire day, but rode like a queen.

Lydia smiled grimly at the thought. No matter what else happened, she felt sure that Siona would never have her will in that matter.

She slept that night only to be awakened by an oppressive air, a feeling of suffocation. She was alone in the tent but felt nervy in an unfamiliar way. Suddenly, she heard distant thunder and whimpered. Thunderstorms had never frightened her before, but somehow the very feel of the air affected her at this altitude. She waited, curled up in a ball, for the rain to begin, but the thunder was never interrupted and the pressure only grew.

After an hour or so, the rumbling finally died away and she relaxed into sleep.

*   *   *

The final summit was unremarkable, merely another high point on the trail. Soon thereafter, the character of the land changed. Granite boulders became more evident, unscreened by clinging moss; the dust of the trail rose in clouds as they rode, undampened by morning mists.

Here and there, the startling yellow of turning aspen groves showed strong against the dull pines, the gold which gave the pass its name. The leaves had yet to fall, and rattled gently in the breeze. Lydia noted, below the trail, the strangely spherical shape of a circle pine, and wished she could grab one of the pinecones for luck.

It was dull riding, and Lydia soon found herself daydreaming, inventing songs that she might never have the opportunity to write down. Her mare took a chance to crop at some of the dried grasses on the verge, huge weedy structures that had been sun-bleached for months. The attendants had fallen silent, and the only sounds were of the horses' hoofbeats.

A line of sweat trickled down the back of Lydia's neck, soon joined by others, making her clothes cling and bind to her. It was absurd that it should be so hot at such an altitude. She wished for a huge floppy hat to screen her head from the sun, one such as peasant women wore. Never noble ladies. Noble ladies wore silly little hatlings that didn't protect the head at all. Noble *men* could wear what they liked, and not risk censure.

Noble men could also indelicately wipe sweat away. Lydia missed her masquerade sometimes.

Something bothered her. It nagged at the ends of her attention. The hoof beats seemed too loud somehow, echoing down the trail. She squinted up at the sun. It was the too-bright of her childhood summers, the sky bleached to a pale, cloudless blue. And it was so very hot, the sort of heat that only came once in a long while. She shook her head and took a drink from her flask. It was water, only water; she didn't feel like drinking anything else.

Her mare started acting up, shying sideways at the lightest touch. Lydia tried to soothe the beast, and the mare gentled but trembled a bit. Lydia frowned. Whatever she was trying to remember was from back at the castle, a memory like an aching tooth. She had told Orrin something, a month or more ago, that was related to what she was seeing now. She felt the thump of the trudging horse shoot all the way up her spine, trying to jar the memory free.

Her heart-rate sped up when she realized what was wrong with what she was seeing. More precisely, it was with what she was hearing. There was no birdsong. The birds had been silent for some time, and she was only now realizing it. Lydia sat a little straighter and looked around; she looked at the tall, dead weeds on the verge, bleached out in the odd light. What was it she had said? Floods at the thaw; plants that grow too large, too quick. Then die. It was the herald of famine.

A deer startled out of the brush and bounded ahead on the trail, to the accompaniment of the startled shouts of the guards. All of the horses were restless now. Lydia barely paid attention to them, or to the smaller creatures that were starting to appear, because she remembered, with heartbreaking clarity, the dry thunder of two days gone and she knew, even before the breeze shifted, exactly what they faced.

Fire.

The light changed, giving the land an orange tint as smoke sculled across the sun. Lydia pulled her mare's head around. "We have to get to the river!" she screamed, and slammed her heels into the mare's sides before anyone could argue, riding off the trail at an angle.

The valley sides were breathtakingly steep for a rider, and more than once her mare stumbled, sliding in the loose duff. Lydia lay low across the bay's neck, reins slack in her hands, and whispered prayers at the jolting descent that she might not fall off, that the mare did not trip, and that no branches were in the way. Soon enough those prayers became no more than an invocation, or an oath.

She couldn't hear anyone behind her over her own gasping breath. After a small eternity of nightmare descent, the trees parted and the mare strode forward into a wondrous wide spot in the river. Lydia dismounted as the mare stepped chest high and found the water up to her own chest.

Looking to the right, past the horse, she saw the pool narrow and abruptly terminate into the open air. The river valley opened up onto another and Lydia found a faint thread of hope. The waterfall churned up air; the wider valley below directed breezes up towards where she stood. With fresh air and water the party might make it through.

The water—none too swift at the end of summer, but powerful for all of that—eddied warm and cold around her. Lydia turned and stopped, transfixed.

Upstream, no more than half a league away, was a scene out of nightmares yet to come. A wall of smoke blocked off the sky to the south, rising to the heavens on the forest holocaust. Trees were aflame, pine and fir and aspen were indiscriminate shadows against the sucking fire. The ground glowed like coals, a line of creeping flames fighting their way against the steady wind from the valley. Lydia could not tear her eyes away.

I had not thought that fires could be so dark. She dropped the reins and watched helplessly as the blaze advanced.

Another rider splashed into the pool. Lydia half-turned, wondering who had managed to follow her so closely and had only a glimpse of the captain of the guard before he grabbed her head and shoved it under the water.

In her disbelief, Lydia exhaled, and then knew she had no breath left to fight the impersonal hand. She wrenched her head *toward* the guard, who lost his grip on her short hair. Doubling up, she pushed off against his knees and cut through the water with the current, putting several lengths between them before putting her feet down.

I am no black hag to sink with a heart of stone, she thought as she rose, crouching a bit so that her head was the only thing above water as she spluttered. Through the streaming water she could see the man advancing on her grimly. He was bigger than her, and stronger. Her only advantage was that he thought she was helpless. *What was his name?* Tuaren. That was it.

One should know the name of the man who comes to kill you, Lydia thought.

Still crouching, she pulled the knife from her belt. After a moment's thought, she switched it to her left hand, under the water, with the blade up. He paused for a moment, just out of reach. Then Tuaren lunged.

Lydia threw her fist in as strong a punch as she could manage. It was slowed by the weight of the water; she connected but he shook it off, grabbing at her arm, wrenching it off to the side. Lydia turned with that twist, bringing her left arm up with the knife. This time the knife went where it was aimed, right to the guard's throat.

Tuaren's eyes widened and she leaned back, pulling straight across. The knife came out in her hand but the guard was already falling, bright red eddies of blood spreading through the pool and down the current. Lydia heard a gasp even over the roar of the fire.

The Lady Siona was on the riverbank, just shy of the water's edge. She looked at the tableau with an expression that Lydia had never seen before. Fear and desolation were warring on her features. Then, she turned her horse in complete panic and lashed the reins across the horse's back. Her horse started, and then began to climb.

"Sunny, no!" screamed Lydia. She struggled towards the riverbank. A rock turned under her foot and she fell, dropping her knife, and losing her footing for a terrifying moment. The falls were close, too close for safety. She stood again, hair streaming over her vision, and when she could see again, the Lady was gone. Lydia paused, shivering, then took another glance at the fire.

A crashing sound heralded the appearance of Siona's attendants, near hysterics, and it took some doing to calm them down and to persuade them into the river. The other guards helped as they could, but were mainly concerned with keeping the horses calm. The air was already filled with ash, and the party had to crouch down to breathe the cooler air over the water. By the time Lydia thought to look, Tuaren's body was already gone, carried over the falls by the current. *River, oh river, carry my troubles away,* she thought crazily. There was no more time for thoughts.

The interlude at the river seemed to take hours. The water, warmed though it was, chilled the party soon enough; the air was full of smoke and ash. They had to keep ducking beneath the water, which was almost as murky as the air, and they choked as the flames surrounded them. Finally the flames passed on, and the party moved to the shallows; it was sunset before the ground was cooled enough to move out of the river. Their camp that night was simple. They had lost the mules that carried their possessions, and what little food they had was soaked. They did not sleep well in their sodden misery, coughing through the night.

They found the Lady Siona in a narrow crevice lined with vines. Her horse was nowhere to be seen. The rock walls had protected her from the fury of the flames but not the smoke; she lay curled on her side, her skirts spread as gracefully as though she had placed them. Her skin was pale, but there were yet roses in her cheeks.

Were it not for the unnatural stiffness of her pose, she might have been sleeping.

"Oh, Sunny," whispered Lydia.

*   *   *

Murky light watched over the much diminished party as the keep came into view. The overcast brought no relief from the heat; the muggy atmosphere was the sort in which tempers frayed to the breaking point.

Lydia couldn't find it in herself to care.

As they approached the gate, she looked up to see the flag of Guardron on its pole, hung next to the green flag and wheat sheaf of Kentwell. *Good*, she thought absently, and stumbled a little. The guards at the gate looked at the party in confusion, and well they should. No one was riding; the chills that the horses had taken from standing in the river had left them but lightly lamed, and Lydia was adamant that they should not damage them by riding further. They were all of them in ruined clothes, smeared with soot and torn from those first few days. They'd had to leave two guardsmen and a maid behind, one at a shepherd's cot and two at an inn. The long immersion had fevered their lungs and one of the guardsmen had developed pneumonia.

The descent had been two long weeks, a journey that should have taken barely five days. They had eaten little in all of that time. It had taken Lydia half that to get the maids to stop weeping.

One of the guards stepped forward to challenge them as they entered the gate. He seemed nervous, unwilling to confront a group so sorely in need, and Lydia squinted up at him uncertainly. He looked back, startled, then swallowed whatever he had been going to say and stammered, "Lady? Um... Lydia? We thought..." He thought better of it, and gathered himself together. "Welcome home, Lady."

Lydia nodded absently, and led her mare toward the opening. Behind her, she heard the hissing as the guard—who must be somebody she should recognize, but she was so weary—explained in an undertone to his companions, one of whom ducked past the trudging party and went to herald her return to the rest of the keep.

The courtyard was a buzz of activity, and Lydia swayed a bit as she stood off to the side. The midnight blue, black, and silver of Guardron was evident on several people; she dimly realized that the famine aid was being run from out of the keep. Guards and merchants were moving around speedily, even in the heat, and Lydia was dizzied by the continual movement. There was a startled lull as the party limped into view, then an excited murmur as people speculated on their appearance. A groom came up and took hold of Lydia's horse, and she remembered to release her grip on the reins. Out of the corner of her eye, she saw the excited guard speaking to a man dressed all in blue and black and she sighed, knowing that she didn't have to hold on too much longer.

Lord Guardron dismissed the guard, then began to walk over to where Lydia stood. "Lady Lydia...?" he asked. She turned and raised her head, and an oath he certainly hadn't meant escaped his lips. *"Alan?"*

"Lydia," she replied firmly, and swallowed. "Duchess of Kentwell." That last was harder to say than she had thought.

Duke Jordeth crossed the remaining distance. He looked her over carefully. "What... what happened? Your party was expected days gone." His gaze reached her feet and he looked up, shocked. "You're barefoot."

Lydia shrugged. "My boots didn't outlast their soaking. We were in the river." She shook her head. "There was a fire..." It was very hard to concentrate. There was something she had to do, wasn't there?

The duke took hold of her shoulders, steadying her. "Where is the Duchess—the Lady Siona?" Lydia looked past him at the final horse, the one carrying the rough travois. A circle of silence fell around the horse and its shrouded burden as its owner led it further into the courtyard. Jord looked at the travois, eyes widening.

Lydia smiled a bitter smile as she remembered what she had to do. *Oh, yes. That was it.* She held herself a little straighter. "Duke Jordeth," she said, drawing his attention back to her. "As the Duchess of Kentwell, it is my right to declare that the death of the Lady Siona is questionable, and as is only fit under the Charter and the laws of Rooke, any confusion regarding her death should be cleared. I hereby formally request that an investigation be made into the events surrounding the death of this noble lady. Let no stone be unturned; let no questions go unanswered; and may this investigation continue until the king himself is satisfied. I ask this in the name of Rooke, and may your inquest be blessed by the Lord and Lady. *Á meren ap domán, le altará.*"

Jord's eyes grew wide as she went through the formula. It hadn't taken much research to discover the phrasing; while the law was seldom implemented, it was a part of the Charter and, as such, taught along with the rest. From the look on the duke's face, he knew precisely what she was asking. "Do you mean this?" he asked, frowning. "If you do this, you will be under as much suspicion as the rest, and I will have to investigate you as well."

"Yes," she replied. It didn't matter anymore; she had no secrets left to hide. A fleeting memory of the struggle in the river made her close her eyes.

"You are certain? We will have to know everything of where you have been, and what you have struggled to keep secret..." he trailed off, looking dubiously at the girl who had so lately been known to him as a boy.

"Yes," she said emphatically. She was tired, so tired. The fingers around her shoulders tightened and she looked up at the Duke.

"This is what you've been planning all along, isn't it," he said, suspicious. "This is exactly what you wanted. *How did you know?"*

Lydia looked up at him, desolated. "I thought it would be me," she murmured. Jordeth dropped his hands and her attention was caught by a movement in one of the stairwells. A nurse stood, carrying an excited small boy who pointed and laughed at the various people in the courtyard. The boy was dressed in green; his hair was bleached gold.

He's so big, Lydia thought distractedly, and then it hit her.

She would have to be the one to tell Mikal that his mother was dead.

With a wail, she broke down in the tears she had been holding back. Duke Jordeth held her, awkwardly, as she sobbed into the front of his shirt and the storm finally broke, sending people scurrying as the downpour began.

He never knew how miraculous either rain was.

Staff of Iron

*Then she has taken a silver sword and given him strokes
three*
*And she's turned him back to the boldest knight that ever
your eyes did see.*
Then she has taken a silver horn and loud and shrill blew she
And all the fish came unto her but the mackerel of the sea
*Saying "You shaped me once an unseemly shape and you'll
never more shape me!"*

Then he has sent unto the wood for vines and for hawthorne
And he has taken that lady gay and there he did her burn.

Lydia looked at the window, streaked with the ceaseless rain, and lit a few candles. *Candles in daylight, yet.* Such a winter to follow such a drought. One might be forgiven for wishing that the rain would break just for a little, or turn to snow. She closed the striker and set it aside, blowing through pursed lips as she looked at the pile on the desk.

Well, she had asked for it.

She didn't like to think about the first few weeks after her return. Lord Guardron, true to his promise, had not been gentle in his questioning. With the shock of recent events—including the stunning realization that she was, in spite of her expectations, still alive— fresh in her mind, and the barely restrained effects of hunger and exposure making themselves known, she had alternated between an extreme depression and a vague bewilderment that caused the folk of the keep to regard her with alarm. The end of each session with Duke Jordeth saw another bout of weeping, though she usually managed to get to her tower rooms before the tears began. It was as though all of her emotions, so long suppressed, sought to express themselves all at once. It was all Lydia could do to weather the storm.

Near the end, Jord had asked her what happened to Tuaren. "I don't know," she had replied. It was her only lie.

Mikal regarded her with that strange fear that small children sometimes have around unknown adults. He'd taken the existence of the Guardron men in stride, but this sister of his was quite frightening. It was only when she'd remembered the existence of her old harp, with its strings tarnished but still playable, that she was able to keep him from hiding behind his nurse.

Jord had warmed to her, one day, after he'd caught her singing gently to the small boy. Lydia remembered how he had pressed her to sing, and said nothing.

Once he was done examining her, Jord had turned to the rest of the keep, and Lydia's relief lasted bare days before boredom set in. Though she was making progress with Mikal—that was the only task she had. Unfortunately, her mood was fragile enough that one sleepless night had sent her, weeping, to the foot of the tower stairs when her thoughts turned in upon themselves.

Not a single person came in answer to Lydia's distress.

A Guardron man was the one to wake her in the morning; the tracks of tears still fresh on her face. He didn't say anything, but the trace of pity in his expression was a small comfort. He had presumably said something to his lord, because Jordeth sought her out that day and asked her opinion on some small matters in the governance of Kentwell. Lydia had gladly seized the chance to be doing something—anything—rather than brooding. When the inquiry hadn't turned up anything concrete after several weeks, she'd asked to take over the rest of governance to free Jordeth up. He'd granted her request with surprising grace.

It had led her to this. Her desk piled high with myriad details that had been overlooked, or put off. She'd been working on these for weeks and the pile never seemed to get any smaller. Mind-numbing as it sometimes was, though, it had salvaged what was left of her emotional stability. That was worth the drudgery.

She worked her way through the pile as swiftly as she could, trying in vain to make the work enjoyable. There was, unfortunately, little of interest in the pile, and certainly nothing of challenge. Lord Guardron had taken care of all of the major issues when he had first arrived. Lydia sighed, and fidgeted with the glass pen, finally laying it on the under-shelf. It promptly rolled to the back.

Lydia reached in after it and stubbed her fingers. She frowned, and pulled the pen out carefully, laying it down again upon one of the shorter stacks of documents. Then she reached into the shelf again, slower this time. Her fingers touched the back well short of where she expected them to.

Curious now (and a little grateful for the diversion), she pushed her chair back and got on the floor, peering into the shelf. It was empty of the odds and ends that so often clutter unused surfaces. Lydia pulled down a candle, holding it away from her frizzled hair. The marks of her fingers showed clearly in the dust.

She replaced the candle and walked her hand along the bottom of the desk. Sure enough, the back of the shelf was a spread hand shy of the back of the desk.

After that, it was a matter of figuring out the catch. In the end it turned out to be nothing more than a matter of working a fingernail under the edge of the false backing and pulling it down, but Lydia was grimly amused at the shock of the maidservant who had found her under the desk, tugging gleefully away. *Ah, well. They probably think I'm a bit touched anyway.*

Lydia bit thoughtfully on the edge of a torn fingernail, and peered back into the shelf. She reached back in, careful as before, and found a small bundle of folded papers. They were stiff but not ancient; Lydia estimated that they were a few years old at least and—

she flexed one that seemed stiffer than the rest—a decade old at most. She felt uneasy.

After a moment, she bit her lip and unfolded the one that seemed oldest. *My lovely autumn sun*, she read, *dearest Rhianna...* Lydia stifled a laugh. All this worry, and she'd done nothing more than stumble across some lover's cache.

Some lover's cache in the work desk of the lady of the keep? she wondered. After a moment, Lydia left the letters in her lap and squared off the pile on her desk, placing it on the floor. Then, she stared at the letters, willing them to be something innocent, perhaps older than she thought they were.

My mother's name was Sarai, she thought, and with a sigh began to read them.

*   *   *

Duke Jordeth found her long after the dinner hour. The candles had long since guttered out and Lydia sat in semi-darkness, lips pressed to the side of one hand as she stared at the letters fanned out across the desk. "What have you got there?" he asked.

Lydia did not turn around. "Proof," she replied, almost curt.

Jord raised his eyebrows. "Proof? There is actually written proof? More fools they." It was a mark of his increased esteem that he did not question her word. "Where did you find these?"

Lydia waved at the desk. "There's a little nook, there..." She trailed off, clenching her hands. "A perfect hiding place for secret letters. Love letters."

"Love letters?" Jord asked, picking one up and starting to read it with a frown.

Lydia took a deep breath. "From Captain Tuaren to the Lady Siona." That had been surprisingly hard to accept, once she'd read them—to think that that dangerous man had such poetry in him. Such music. There were paeans to his love that Lydia could write songs from, and then his other nature would assert itself, telling blandly of "obstacles removed."

Beautiful words in the soul of a killer.

"Siona? But this says Rhianna," Jord replied in a sharpened tone.

"She was lying to my father all along," Lydia returned, voice quavering. She sorted through the pile. "Here, this one mentions it."

Lord Guardron took the letter, read it silently, and pressed his lips together. "She was at the heart of it, then?"

"She and Tuaren both. I had thought..." Lydia shook her head. "I had hoped otherwise. But I never understood her."

"The lady and her lover," Jord muttered. He froze. "Since... before she met your father?" he asked, a new note in his voice.

Lydia closed her eyes. It had been a forlorn hope that sharp-eyed Duke Jord would not notice that. She nodded, once.

"Then Mikal..."

"Is the only family I have left," Lydia overrode him quietly. She turned to him, eyes pleading. "There is no way to know for certain."

"He looks nothing like your father."

"He looks just like his mother," Lydia countered.

Jordeth looked at her, eyes narrowing. "You'd accept that? Knowing that he could be a bastard?"

Her laugh was mirthless. "Instead of brother to one traitor, and son of another? Oh, I know, my Lord Guardron," she persisted when he shook his head, "my father was never thought to be a traitor. But I know what he planned," she finished, a bleak note in her voice.

Jord held still for a long moment. "What would you have me do?" he asked, quietly.

"Send these to the king," she replied. "He needs to know."

"And after?" he asked, almost gently.

Lydia bowed her head. "Say what you will, Duke. Kentwell should be told. But leave me a brother, if you can."

Jord gathered up the letters. "If I can," he repeated.

*   *   *

Lydia wedged herself into an archer's slit, sticking her nose out into the crisp air. The overcast had finally burnt off, and though the day was still cold, there was actual sunshine to be seen. And here she was, still in the keep. She wriggled back out, smoothed her skirts, and then glanced up and down the hall. She saw no one, and a smile played around the edges of her lips.

In truth, it shouldn't please her that so many of the servants and guards had given notice in the wake of the inquiry. Some were offended by the questioning, some by the revealed behavior of the late Lady Siona. Some, no doubt, did not care for Lydia and her "southern" notions of governance. But Lydia was grateful that Siona's picked confidants and cronies would not stay around to plague her.

Spring was on its way. She hiked up her skirts and started running down the corridor.

She flew past a pair of guards, whose startled expressions she caught out of the corner of her eye. She pulled one hand free to catch the corner of the wall, and ran straight to the doorway of the study that Guardron still used. She stopped abruptly, panting, when she realized that Jordeth was not alone.

Two men looked up at the lady clinging to the doorway, and the man with the red and gold badge—a messenger—stood and bowed to her. Lord Guardron covered his mouth with a hand, as though he were suppressing a smile. Lydia nodded to the messenger and folded her hands in an attempt to look demure.

"Lady Minstrel," the messenger said, rising.

Lydia's smile grew bewildered. "Yes...?" She couldn't have heard that right.

Jordeth said, calmly, "We were just about to send for you."

The messenger nodded. "Lady Kentwell. I have a packet for you, Duchess." He pulled out a bulging leather folder and extended it towards her. She took it, uncertainly. His eyes were shining.

"And the rest?" Duke Jord prompted. The messenger jumped, as though startled. "Oh, yes. Lady Lydia, Duchess of Kentwell, the king has formally invested you in charge of your duchy, and grants this patent of arms as your personal sigil." He extended a rolled parchment, which Lydia unrolled slowly. It was the Kentwell arms, surely, but there was a vine wrapped around the wheat sheaf, and an inscription below. "En vara fijende," she murmured. *Ivy, of course. The faithful vine.*

The messenger was still staring at her. She smiled at him, uneasily, and he looked as though he were a puppy she'd praised. What in the world had he heard about her? "I thank you," she said formally. She might have gone on, but she didn't even know his name, and he looked almost ecstatic that she'd acknowledged him.

"It is my duty, Duchess," he replied shyly, and bowed his way out of the room. Lydia bit her lip and turned to Guardron. "My lord, what was that about?" she asked. Jord spread his hands by way of reply. "I suppose that he was tongue-tied in the presence of a pretty young Duchess," he said.

Lydia put the patent down, and turned the folder over in her hands. "I wonder..." she said, and opened it to find a stack of paper. She sat and read the first sheet. She quickly flipped to the next, eyebrows rising, then began to laugh as she thumbed through the stack. Jord looked on patiently, but after some time had passed, inquired, "What is it?"

"Ballads," Lydia laughed, and handed some over to the duke. "Ballads about the King's Minstrel."

Jord sat back, frowning thoughtfully at the pages in his hand. " 'I shall do your will, sire, So long as you ne'er Look into my past.' What manner of nonsense are they talking about?"

"Is it any sillier than The Ratcatcher, or Lazy Maidens Catch the Fish?" Lydia passed a few more sheets over. " 'Bred in treachery to be true,' now there's a wretched line to sing." She uncovered the last sheets and stopped, smile softening. She read this one closely.

Jord stated, absently, "He's a bright one, our king. If these are what they're singing in Ellidar, it won't be long before the rest of Rooke follows suit." He stopped, noting Lydia's inattention. "What have you got there?"

Lydia smiled, still reading. "This one's for me," she replied.

Ever After

Spring

Lydia sat on the broad windowsill and leaned her head against the frame. From here, she could see the foothills below the keep, and catch a glimpse of the great valley below. The farmland that was even now being planted with the seed saved by the supplies of Guardron. The river was running at its normal levels; the snowpack did not seem to be melting unduly fast. The likelihood was that this would be a bountiful year.

She spread her hand along the hinges. The air was so clear today. No haze or fog was visible. Kentwell spread out below her like a child's plaything. She could imagine that she could see to its very end, so far north. The Lady Duchess gave a small laugh.

Here she was, up in her tower suite, when she should be down below with the visitors. The sudden press of too many people had never seemed to bother her before. She'd almost choked and had fled at the first opportunity.

"I have done with lies," she said quietly. It was not the press of people that had frightened her so. Nor was it the royal procession, the first in five years. It was the king. He'd greeted her as formally as he should, as formally as she'd received him. All winter, she had been wondering what their first meeting would be like. Now... well, she was scared.

She paused and sat up a little straighter. No. She should not be afraid. There was nothing to be afraid of. The king would treat her well enough, and if he didn't... she looked down and a wry smile crossed her lips.

If another noble lady thought of going out the window, she probably wouldn't expect to survive the experience.

A knock at the door caught her by surprise. She turned, realized who it was, and said, "Enter," with only a little uncertainty in her voice.

The king entered, alone, a bit breathless. Lydia looked past him, expecting at least a servant. Taking a deep breath she said uncertainly, "Greetings, your majesty."

He burst out laughing, and when she looked at him, he choked out, "*William*, remember?" She covered her mouth with her hand, but when she took it away, no hint of a smile crossed her features. The king sobered, and said, "Jord is willing to aver that he and I have been discussing the aid project, if you were wondering." He took a deep breath. "That is far too many stairs."

Lydia did smile, then. "I chose these rooms when I was a girl, because every princess in every tale lived in a tower. I kept them because I was stubborn. Eighty-nine stairs, if you were wondering."

"I... yes," he gasped, then collected himself. "I should like your advice," he said, smiling.

Lydia leaned back against the windowsill, an ironic smile on her face. "Really?"

He nodded. "I find that I will need you to fulfill your promise," and as Lydia blinked in confusion, he continued, "You once promised you should sing at my wedding feast."

Lydia tilted her head. "I did. I shall, if you would like. But I will need to know when your wedding is to be."

"There is my difficulty." William had a small grin on his face, half rueful, as though he expected to get a scolding for something he was pleased about. Lydia refused to speculate. She spread her hands in an invitation to continue. "I find... well, I am not sure how to ask the lady."

Lydia felt a strong surge of irritation, and kept it out of her voice as she said, "And you would like my advice on how to do this?"

William looked at his feet. "Actually, I should like an answer."

Lydia had her mouth open for a reply when the actual import of his words hit her. She turned her initial query into, "You *know* I am the last person you should marry..."

He raised his head. "Why?"

Because...

Lydia stared off into the center of the room. There were reasons. Surely there were reasons. But every reason she brought to mind evaporated. She found herself looking at William in dawning comprehension. He was grinning with an oddly fond look on his face, and he said, softly, "I think I will remember that look for the rest of my life."

Lydia took a short breath, thought better of what she was going to say, and held out her hand. William clasped her fingers, gently, and said, "Minstrel Alan, speechless? Wondrous doings in Kentwell."

"Lydia," she insisted, then realized the absurdity of the two of them, speaking their own names more than the other's. She giggled. William, still holding her hand, slid down onto the windowsill next to her. "Lydia, the King's Minstrel," he murmured, still watching her face. "*Queen* Minstrel."

Lydia held absolutely still for a moment. "Hold. I... well... queen?"

William raised an eyebrow. "That is part of marrying a king," he said.

"Oh," she replied. "Mmm."

He quirked his eyebrow, "Strange that you should find that to be so hard." He looked past her shoulder and caught the view. "This is the window?"

Lydia took a breath. "Yes, this is the window."

"It's a long way down."

She smiled then, a genuine relieved smile. "A very long way down." She reached out and pulled the shutter to.

9 7 8 1 9 4 0 9 3 8 7 8 3